Shawty
So Weak for That
Thug Love

A NOVEL BY

SUNNI NYKOHL

Curvy Girl Publications is now accepting manuscripts from aspiring & experienced BBW romance authors!

WHAT MAY PLACE YOU ABOVE THE REST:

Heroes who are the ultimate book bae: strong-willed, maybe a little rough around the edges but willing to risk it all for the woman he loves.

Heroines who are the ultimate match: the girl next door type, not perfect - has her faults but is still a decent person. One who is willing to risk it all for the man she loves.

The rest is up to you! Just be creative, think out of the box, keep it sexy and intriguing!

If you'd like to join the Curvy Girl family, send us the first 15K words (60 pages) of your completed manuscript to curvygirlpub@royalty-publishinghouse.com

ACKNOWLEDGMENTS

This book was inspired by one of the most charming people I have ever met. Your constant encouragement and supportive nature fueled me on days where I just wanted to give up. Thank you for placing the batteries in my back and supplying the spiritual energy I needed to see this through. Though none are perfect when we acknowledge our mistakes we give ourselves the chance to grow and become better than we were yesterday.

Thank you

SYNOPSIS

Sadie and LaNoir, college soros, appeared to have hit the jackpot when it came to their relationships with homeboys, Reggie "Mad Maxx" Montana and Brooklyn "B-Boy" Thompson, but things aren't always what they seem to be. LaNoir, a true firecracker, sparked Sadie's interest in her lover, Brooklyn when she spilled the juicy details of their kinky sex life proving some things shouldn't be shared between friends. Sadie knows her growing lust for Brooklyn is the last thing she should be focused on but how could she ignore the sexy, aggressive nature he possesses when Reggie's gentle spirit didn't satisfy her the way she knew Brooklyn could. Against their better judgment Sadie and Brooklyn cross known boundaries when they allow their mutual attraction to spill over their pot of brewing lust. Concealing the fact that you had mind-blowing sex with your best friend's mate turns out to be the least of their worries. How does it feel when the tables turn, and you find out your partner has secrets of their own?

CHAPTER 1

*I*t was 6:47 pm and he was seventeen minutes late by the time he'd arrived for our scheduled rendezvous. The coffee shop we'd agreed upon was in an out of the way spot, not too far from downtown. It used to be a popular diner a year or so ago, but I guess as the saying goes 'all good things must come to an end.' I wasn't impressed by the changes made by new owners. Maybe it was the new paint that coated the walls; I've never been a fan of the color green.

The new paint choice was just a small distraction from the thoughts swimming through my head. I'd spent hours carefully picking my outfit for the evening. I didn't want to seem too anxious or overly sexy so anything with cleavage exposure was absolutely out of the question. I contemplated wearing a tangerine skirt that clung to my ass like Velcro, but that wouldn't be much better if I wanted the attention focused on my mind rather my extremely curvy frame. I wanted his attention, but I didn't want to come across as super obvious either. I settled on a simple red, cotton top and a pair of dark denim bottoms; that choice would scream friendship instead of the lusty thoughts that had been brewing over the past few days. I made sure to grab my favorite scarf as well.

Brooklyn was something special. He was six-foot-four, slim build, with a little lighter than caramel complexion, and had a special shade of brown eyes that set off fireworks when the light hit them just right. He was heavily tatted, and I secretly wanted to lick each and everyone; especially the one on his neck that read *Warrior*.

"Sadie?" he said as he approached.

"Oh, so you don't know me now?" I joked as he sat across from me.

"Nah, it has been a while though. I'm glad you decided to meet with me tonight." He smiled, and I noticed two dimples I'd never witnessed before. Maybe it had been that long.

"Indeed, it has. I'm liking the new look," I referenced his locs that were tied neatly on his head. Maybe it was because of the context which we were meeting that made him look like a delicious ice cream cone on a hot-ass day even though it was the middle of December. I wanted to lick all over him and savor his flavor. I could imagine his cream coating my mouth and sliding down my throat, but I couldn't let that be known…at least not right away.

Brooklyn and I were playing a game that had real potential to cause a few people a tremendous amount of pain. We both belonged to someone else yet here we were, portraying as if this meeting was just two old friends playing catch up. If that was really true we would have invited his wife, my soror and my husband, his ex-bandmate. We were all college friends who slowly ended up parting ways due to life mixed with a few secrets. Six years later Brooklyn and I find ourselves here, sitting at this little wooden table in an out of the way shop, stirring up coffee as well as old feelings.

Brooklyn 'B-Boy' Thompson was every bit of a lady's man back in our early college days. He was full Emirati and he embraced his heritage even though the majority of his family had become Americanized since migrating over. He was the big man on campus; him and my husband Reggie 'Mad Maxx' Montana. Back then Brooklyn and Reggie had the party scene on lock. Every major college show and even local clubs booked D.T.A.- Death to Average.

"What are you mixed with?" I asked as I twirled my fingers in Reggie's short, black curly hair. We'd just left Platinum Paradise where D.T.A. had shut the club down with their live performance. They were the hottest out of the three booked performers to hit the stage that night. Reggie had invited me and my crew to watch them perform at the swanky club after a few days of flirting via text. He wasn't the type of guy I'd normally be attracted to as far as looks were concerned, but he wasn't ugly by far. He was just a little vanilla style and personality wise for my taste.

He was about six-foot even, two hundred pounds of cinnamon colored goodness. He wore black, box styled glasses more than he wore his contacts and his coils were soft and wild on his head. He used to have braces, so his teeth were perfectly positioned when he smiled. I was accustomed to guys with more edge than Reggie possessed, but he was still sexy. I liked tattoos, cornrows, and men that wore gold fronts. I wanted a neatly trimmed, bearded man that bit his lip in his pictures.

"Mixed? Why a black man gotta be mixed to have curly hair?" he replied looking over his frames like a professor questioning his student.

"Look don't start with me, Reggie. I know you and your boys are 'woke' and what not but I just wanna know your ethnicity that's all. Most black men around here don't have hair like yours," I defended my question.

"My father is Arabian, and my mother is originally from Botswana; she moved here as a baby though. They met while my father was in the service," he answered as he placed his hand on my leg. "Yo', I like these leggings," he complimented and squeezed my thigh.

"They are the same hot pink leggings we all are wearing," I laughed and pointed at the rest of my sorors. I pulled on the bottom of my green and pink tee. "I guess you like my shirt too, huh?" I smiled as I moved his hand off my thigh.

"Yea, they're cute in their lil' pants but you… you got that booty and them thighs that make you stand out amongst the crowd." He smiled.

"Don't start trying to sweet talk me, boy." I giggled.

"Why not? It's working. You weren't smiling like this before I came over and sat with you, and I know because I was watching you from the stage." He peered over his glasses again.

"Oh, you were watching me?" I smirked.

"Fa sho. Look B-Boy and I are about to grab something to eat. You tryna ride or…" The offer was for me as well as my best friend LaNoir. She was a bit of a firecracker. You know the type, loud but beautiful. She was brown skin, about five-six with a solid frame. She wasn't fat, but she could stand to lose a few pounds for the style of clothing she liked to wear. LaNoir was flashy; the all eyes on me kind of chick who would wear whatever and say whatever at any given minute. She was unpredictable, and I guess that's what Brooklyn liked about her. They'd been inseparable ever since he'd seen her blank on a chick at one of his shows. She was the reason I was sitting beside Reggie right now. She'd given him my number without my consent and he'd been blowing up my line ever since.

Reggie was a good guy and I needed a break from the roughneck types I'd usually let sample my goodies. I had plenty of so-called boyfriends throughout my years at North Carolina A &T University, but nothing that ever lasted longer than a few months at a time. I was so tempted to curve Reggie's heavily texting ass, but LaNoir suggested I try something different to get a different result. After consideration, I agreed that she was right. I needed a change from what was familiar and gave Reggie 'Mad Maxx' Montana a real try.

"So, how'd you get the name, Mad Maxx?" I asked Reggie as the waitress handed me my refill of orange juice.

"You didn't know ya boy is a lyrical genius? When he gets in his zone it's like he catches the holy ghost of rhymes," Brooklyn interjected.

4

"I go crazy on the mic." Reggie smirked. I noticed he added a ton of salt to his bowl of grits. I was super observant, always noticing the details that seemed to bypass everyone else.

"Where's that mutha fuckin' waitress at!" LaNoir barked.

"What's the problem?" Brooklyn questioned.

"I told her I wanted my steak well done, this mutha fuckah pink in the middle!" she exclaimed with disgust pouring from her lips.

"Well we can just send it back," Brooklyn suggested in hopes of calming LaNoir down. We've been kicked out of too many places because of her nasty attitude. She could be a real gem to those that took the time to see past her rough edges but getting there was a trip most people didn't want to take.

"Excuse me! Ex-cuuuse mee!" LaNoir started to shout at the stocky, blonde-haired woman with the dark roots that had taken our order. "Um, I asked for my steak to be well done. Does this look well done to you?" LaNoir picked up a piece of the undercooked meat and held it close to waitress's face.

"Really, LaNoir?" I thought it was very rude of her to take out her food frustrations on the waitress. Shit, she wasn't the chef. All she did was take the order.

"Naw, she needs to see that this ain't what the fuck I asked for!" LaNoir snapped.

"I can take it back ma'am and ask that it be cooked a little longer," the waitress suggested.

"Yea well you do that and take the rest while you're at it because it's gonna need to be reheated as well," LaNoir insisted as she slid the rest of her food to the edge of the table. The waitress grabbed the plates and hurried off into the kitchen.

"Damn girl, you could have been a lil' nicer." I shot a frown at LaNoir.

"It's okay, I bet they will get the order right this time." She turned and faced Brooklyn. "So, listen we are having our annual Christmas party in a few weeks and we were wondering if B-Boy and Mad Maxx would come thru?"

"You were wondering, Sadie?" Reggie addressed me.

5

"Huh?" I replied, even though I'd heard him clearly.

"She just said y'all wanted to know if D.T.A. could make a special appearance. I'm asking if pretty Sadie with the honey eyes wants Maxx to come and see her at her event?"

"Only if he wears a Santa suit." I smirked.

"A Santa suit? Yo', is this a costume party?" He sat up and laughed. He had a beautiful smile.

"Yes, it's a Christmas party so everyone has to come in character." I smiled.

"That's what's up. We'll be there." He licked his lips like LL Cool J. It wasn't long before LaNoir had her steaming hot food and we were all enjoying our meals. I noticed Brooklyn laid a hefty tip on the table which was well deserved after LaNoir's rude-ass behavior. Even though LaNoir was my girl I often wondered what Brooklyn saw in her besides her physical beauty. It seemed like she was forever causing him some type of public embarrassment.

Sadie stop hatin'! That's your girl, be happy for her, I thought as I watched them kiss goodbye when they dropped us off at the dorm. I was so engulfed in their romance I was startled when Reggie leaned in for a kiss. I reluctantly gave him what he was seeking, but I didn't give him any tongue. Reggie was definitely a good guy, but with 'B-Boy' Brooklyn was where I secretly wanted to be.

CHAPTER 2

*C*onversation between Reggie and I thickened over the next few weeks. He would make someone a great husband one day; the problem was I wasn't looking for a husband. I wanted to experience passion in its rawest form and from what LaNoir constantly told me about Brooklyn, he was what I wanted. She'd brag consistently about how good he'd suck her pussy and how he'd stuff her to capacity with his heavy meat until she'd beg for him to stop. If I had Brooklyn between my thighs I wouldn't beg for his release, I'd beg for more.

I knew it was wrong for me to think about my best friend's man in that sense, but deep down if given the chance I'd fuck Brooklyn with no remorse. LaNoir was just a pretty face, with no real substance or value. Brooklyn was too much man for a loud, hood chick, even though he was street ready himself. He needed a woman with class and sophistication on his arm to complement his stature. He needed someone to round out his rough edges not make them sharper. He needed me.

We all agreed to go shopping for our costumes together. We hit up Costume Magic in our local mall. "I don't want to be all grandma-ish. Look at this shit," LaNoir complained as she exited the dressing room looking extremely matronly in her Mrs. Clause attire. "You can't even see my titties in this shit!" She pulled at her bust line trying to expose her cleavage.

"Aw, it's not that bad," I lied. She looked completely horrible in that ensemble, but I secretly wanted to show her up in hopes of gaining Brooklyn's attention.

"You're used to wearing shit like this," LaNoir said as she wiggled around trying to find comfort in the unflattering piece.

"And what is that supposed to mean?" I crinkled my nose at her remark. Sure, I wasn't a size five, but I wore my weight well and dressed appropriately. I was sexy and classy, unlike LaNoir who always had on something a size too small for her pudgy build.

"Nothing girl, I just meant that you don't mind being covered. I got to keep it spicy for B-Boy with all these lil' hoes that be in his face after he performs. Shit, if I don't keep some tricks up my sleeve to keep his mind focused on me, I'm sure one of those skanks would be all over his dick in no time." She started to disrobe.

"Well, what you do girl? Like I'm not tryna be all in your business or anything but if he's friends with Reggie you know what they say, birds of a feather…" I conspired to find out everything about Brooklyn's wants and desires so that I could become the object of his affection. As bad as it sounded, LaNoir couldn't possibly be satisfying Brooklyn the way I could if she had to keep coming up with new tricks in the bedroom.

"Oh, you don't have to worry about Reggie, he's a good guy. You don't ever have to worry about doing anything extra with him. Brooklyn said he's all about longevity, romance and all that sap shit." She shrugged. "But B-Boy is crazy kinky girl! He likes all kinds of extra shit. He's been tryna get me to bring another girl into the bedroom, but I dunno if I'm down for all that." She slid her thick thighs into her stonewashed jeans.

"You down with the girl on girl shit?" I was surprised to hear that from her. LaNoir had never given me a reason to think she was gay or bisexual. Or maybe she was bi-curious, seeing that she hadn't actually been with a female.

"I mean… I prefer dick all day, but if that's what he wants I'll be down with the get down. She has to be pretty though, and she definitely has to be into me more than him. I don't want any bitch thinking she can weasel her way into my spot. B-Boy is mine and always will be, trust that." She laughed with her tongue out and raised her hand to give me a high five. *Slap!* I hit her hand and proceeded to get dressed. I silently replayed all the things she said about Brooklyn and I made a mental note to use it all to my advantage. LaNoir was in love with B-Boy, but I wanted Brooklyn.

Hey player, what you gonna get her for Christmas? Girl, what you gonna get that boy? 'Quad City DJ's 12 Ghetto Days of Christmas' blasted from the speakers as Reggie and I walked into the party. I was supposed to be there earlier to help with the decorations, but I wanted to make sure my plan to get Brooklyn's attention was executed perfectly. The room was decked out Christmas style with wreaths, stockings and even mistletoe hanging in the corners of the room. I immediately saw my squad onstage screaming the lyrics to the hood classic. "Come on bitch! 'Bout time you showed up!" LaNoir yelled as I approached. I scanned the room looking for Brooklyn. He was by the bar in his Santa suit which wasn't far from the stage, so I figure this would be the best time to make my presence known.

"I'mma go on stage with my girls, can you put my coat up please?" I asked Reggie as I unbuttoned my black, thigh length pea coat.

"Damn baby!" Reggie's mouth dropped once he saw what I was concealing underneath. While I did purchase the matronly garment LaNoir had heavily complained about, I decided to take my costume in a different direction after hearing the details she spewed about Brooklyn's kinky desires. I was going to be the sexiest elf anyone had ever seen tonight. I wanted to be Santa's dirty little secret. Reggie decided to be a Rudolph once he heard about my costume change, not that it mattered. I didn't give a rat's ass about our matching attire. I wanted to be in the spotlight, but for all the wrong reasons. This was the first time they would see me looking like a pile of lust as I walked up the stairs onto the stage.

"No, you didn't!" LaNoir rolled her neck. "Oh shit, I see you! Reggie got you wide open tonight, huh?" LaNoir yelled as she looked me up and down. I must admit I was super slutty with my red lace bodysuit and black thigh high boots. I had a super short, red velvet skirt on that barely covered my ass cheeks with white fur trim, complete with the elf hat and a big, gold buckle belt. I was a like a shark in the water and Brooklyn was on the menu.

I managed to make it on stage for the very last part of the song and I made sure that all my booty rocking was in Brooklyn's direction. "I want 12 hundred dollars, 11 pairs of shoes, 10 fingernails, 9 packs of weaves, 8 male strippers, 7 bus passes, 6 diamond rings, 5 months free rent, 4 bangles, 3 pocketbooks, 2 earrings, and a man with a lot of money!" We all sang in unison. After the song was over LaNoir took the mic, "Yo' what's up? Next to the stage is our very own, D.T.A.! Y'all show some love for Mad Maxx and my man, B-Boooy!" The place was packed, and the crowd went wild. Everyone knew when D.T.A. was in the building it was sure to go down. The rest of my sorors scattered about as Reggie took the stage with Brooklyn following. I conveniently brushed Brooklyn's arm with my ass cheeks as I pretended to mess with the speakers.

"Shit." He shot me a glanced as he smirked then kept walking. Reggie was truly in beast mode; as he transformed into Mad Maxx on the mic I used his focus to my advantage by flirting with Brooklyn through body language. Everyone was drinking and tipsy by now, so no one paid any attention to my overly seductive dance moves... no one but Brooklyn. He was looking right at me, catching every signal I was throwing, and that's exactly what I wanted. I had his attention and didn't give a damn in that moment if anyone would've noticed. I was on a mission and I would not fail. I wanted him to know that he could get the pussy if he wanted, all he had to do was keep his mouth closed so it would be easier on the both of us.

As the song finished I exited the stage and went to the bar. The guys continued to perform and LaNoir joined me a few minutes later. "Dang chick, I see you going hard for Reggie, huh?" she questioned.

"What?" I heard her words clearly, but I was focused on my next move to have Brooklyn sweating with his pants around his ankles. I wanted to see how heavy his dick really was, and I wasn't going to let LaNoir or Reggie deter me from my target. Yeah, I know I was a horrible friend, but it was just sex. If LaNoir didn't want me to sample the goods, then she should have kept her mouth closed about how great his head game and stroke was.

"You went full streetwalker with your costume. You look good I'm just kinda surprised because you act like you wasn't checking for Reggie," she stated.

"Who said I dressed up for Reggie?" I snapped.

"Well, shit bitch I just assumed." She shrugged. "Who else would you be dressing up for?" She gave me the side eye.

"Why can't I just want to feel good about myself for a night. Everything I do doesn't have to be for a man's attention." I raised my eyebrow, giving her the stank face.

"Sadie don't even try to play me. You've never worn anything remotely similar to this so excuse me for thinking Reggie finally made an impression on your overly-hard-to-please-ass." She scoffed. "But whatever, do you. I just commented on an obvious observation. I have to go get ready for the surprise I have for B-Boy anyway." She sashayed away, walking behind the bar where her pocketbook was hidden.

Surprise? I thought. I wanted to know what she had planned for my future fuck buddy. "A surprise... what kind of surprise?" I called out

"Yeah, girl. He said he wanted me to choose a chick for him tonight. He wants me to be his little freak and bring him a girl like Usher talked about." She smirked as she retrieved her keys from her bag and walked towards the exit. I didn't know what she had up her sleeve, but I did know that while she was absent this would be the perfect time to secure my plan to make Brooklyn want to stuff that heavy pipe of his deep into my walls. The guys were on their third song, so I knew they'd be coming off the stage in a few minutes. I looked at the reflection of myself in the wall mirror beside the bar and thought, *Damn Sadie, you are sexy as fuck and Brooklyn would be a fool to pass up a classy-ass bitch like you. Work your black magic girl and secure that dick tonight.*

As D.T.A. exited the stage I sexy walked my way to where the guys were standing. "Y'all were great! I'm glad I got to see Mad Maxx tonight," I lied as I cuffed my arm around Reggie's waist, giving him a quick hug. I didn't give a shit about Reggie's lyrics. I can't lie, he really was gifted on the mic though, but I'd become slightly obsessed with visuals of Brooklyn sucking on my pussy lips. Reggie could've had rainbows shooting from his mouth and it wouldn't have phased me in the least.

"Thanks, babe. You lookin' hella good tonight too! Shat! You're gonna let me see how that bodywork tonight?" he flirted, and I cringed on the inside when I felt his grasp tighten. I had to play this to my advantage while LaNoir was absent. I wrapped my arms around his neck as I spoke but directed my eyes to Brooklyn.

"Somebody's gonna give me that work tonight." I licked my lips and didn't blink. I was sure Brooklyn was catching all the heat I was throwing at him. He pulled his phone out and tapped it, signaling for me to get my phone while Reggie wasn't paying attention. "Hey babe let me go get my bag. I need to check my lipstick," I lied again.

"You look beautiful, you don't need anything," Reggie complemented and gripped me tighter.

"Thanks, it'll just be a second." I pulled away from him, prying his fingers off my side. I walked with an extra twist in my hips so that my booty bounced with every step that I took. I knew both would be watching as I made my cheeks jiggle and I surely wanted Brooklyn to imagine himself gripping and sliding between these juicy brown rounds. I checked my phone and boom, just as I thought; there it was, a text from Brooklyn. I wondered how he'd gotten my number, but I guess it was probably passed through him to get to Reggie, so I shrugged off the slight concern.

You're playing with fire. I read then replied.

Scared you're gonna get burned? I hit send and was anxious to see his response.

Beep! *Brooklyn: Nah, just tryna figure out your angle.*

No games, just one night if Santa can keep a secret.

Brooklyn: Oh Santa's secrets are the best.

Well if you can keep a secret then what's up?

Brooklyn: Meet me in the coat room in 10

My nipples tingled as I read his last message. I was gonna fuck Brooklyn tonight and I didn't care that he opted for the coat-room. Hell, LaNoir said he liked that kinky shit anyway so I figured why not give him something to remember.

CHAPTER 3

I closed my phone when I saw Reggie approaching. "How long are you trying to be here? Shit to be honest as good as you're looking right now I just want to get out of here and let this red nose glow on ya." His line was extremely corny and only made me want his friend even more. I looked up to see Brooklyn still on his phone.

Fuck it! I thought. I had to figure out a way to curve Reggie before LaNoir's clingy-ass came back from whatever mission she was on. If she came back before Brooklyn had a chance to meet me in the coat-room, Santa wouldn't have a secret to keep.

"That sounds like a plan. I promised LaNoir I'd help with a few things before I left though, so give me a few minutes to find her and see what needs to be done. We should be outta here in like thirty to forty minutes tops, *mmkay?*" I played him to the left and scanned the room one last time to make sure no one was paying any attention as I glided off to the coat-room.

Here and waiting. I texted Brooklyn after I'd eased into the closet. It had just enough room for us to get busy and just enough coats and sweaters to muffle the noise; not mention the music that was still blasting.

Beep! He'd texted back; *I want you to find a scarf and cover your eyes with it.*

A scarf? What the hell kinda game did he want to play? I thought to myself. *How kinky is this nigga?* I wondered as I searched for a scarf that was usable. I found a red, black, and white plaid one and texted him back. *I found one, you coming or what?*

Brooklyn: Omw, but you have to make sure your eyes are covered. I want you to become my sexy secret.

As creepy as that sounded I have to confess that it was also a turn on. I was indeed wanting and willing to be his secret lover for the night, so I tied the scarf around my eyes and waited anxiously. It was only a few seconds later when I heard the door open. "What took you so long?" I joked

"*Shhh...* turn around and don't say another word. I want you from the back since you like to rub your ass against people," he whispered.

I did as I was told. The anticipation was thick. I could feel my pussy moisten from the excitement. *Rrrrip!* He tore a hole in my lace bodysuit after lifting my mini skirt. I gasped as he slid a finger into my warm peach delight. "*Ooo,* you've been wanting this haven't you?" He shoved two fingers in deep and whispered in my ear as he created a rhythm with his stroke.

"*Mmm-hmm,*" I whimpered.

"*Ooo,* yeah I've been wanting to see how this pussy works too," he said in a low, raspy voice, twirling his fingers and flicking my clit. "You know what I want now? I want you to gap them thighs open, so I can get a full view of that pussy." I obliged his request and leaned against the wall for balance. "*Mmm,* look at that. I need to know what that tastes like." He rubbed my clit vigorously, causing me to moan in pleasure.

I felt his soft tongue ease unto my pearl as he began to suck softly. I couldn't have been more excited to have this fine-ass man suckling at my juice box. "You know what's next don't you?" he spoke softly. I knew, and I wanted it terribly. I wanted to finally have his dick digging deep into my now dripping pussy. I heard him adjusting and I gasped when I felt his dick slide into me. His dick was larger than I'd expected. It was almost unbearable. I whimpered as he stroked, but that helpless sound quickly turned into painful moans. I was grateful for the music still blaring outside, and for the coats that lined the walls; they served as the perfect muffler.

"You like big dicks huh? Yeah, you like being stuffed with logs of meat, don't you? I wanna see you take all that dick!" Brooklyn's excitement grew as he spoke. His rhythm seemed to be all over the place. He kept switching from slow strokes to fast. He'd go deep then switch to short strokes causing his oversized pipe to pop out. I tried reaching for it to help guide him back inside, but he grabbed my wrist so forcefully it hurt. "Keep your fucking hands front and center! You've wanted me to give you some dick all night, so I don't need you helping me. Keep your pretty-ass bent over and take this dick!" he demanded.

I must have offended him in some way because he showed no mercy after that. *Bam, bam, bam, bam!* He fucked me hard with no emotion. I couldn't even hear him breathe. Heck, maybe that was because my own voice was covering his. Even though I felt like I was being punished I couldn't help but to smile on the inside. I finally got what LaNoir kept bragging about and that shit turned me on so much a tear fell from my eye when I came. I creamed up and gushed all over his stalk with no remorse and just as quickly as we'd found our way into the coat-room he was gone.

I couldn't even tell if he'd came, he just pulled his dick out and left as soon as I climaxed. I pulled the scarf down from my eyes and let it hang around my neck then adjusted my clothing. I grabbed my coat, deciding to keep the scarf as a souvenir from the night's special event. I had accomplished my goal; fucking the man I'd been infatuated with since the day we met. I smiled as I slipped out into the hallway; peeping out, making sure there was no one to witness my exit.

"Where are you going?" Reggie's voice paralyzed me with fear. "Are you ready?" I heard him say as I tried to walk out of the building unnoticed. I knew I was every bit of foul and even though I had completed my ho-ish task I didn't want to further my 'heauxism' by being in Reggie's face. After all, I did just get dicked-down by his best friend and bandmate.

Damn Sadie, why'd you have to give in to your hoe spirit? You could have just subdued Yoni's throbbing by finally letting Reggie's goody-two-shoe ass eat your pussy like he's been begging to do for the past few weeks, I thought as I turned around slowly. "FUCK!" I couldn't help but say loudly when I saw Reggie standing in front of me with Brooklyn to the right of him and LaNoir cuddled under his arm. She was cheesing like she had her arm cuffed around a trophy.

"What's wrong sweet thang? I thought you wanted to leave together?" Reggie addressed my awkward outburst.

"I'm good. I'm just... I'm just hungry and my feet are hurting from these shoes," I lied. The pain in my face was real, it just wasn't caused by my six-inch boots.

"Okay well shit, we can all go get something to eat then." Reggie indirectly invited Brooklyn and LaNoir to tag along.

"Um, actually I got some leftovers I can warm up. I'm just really tired and want to call it a night," I lied again. There was no way I wanted to sit across from my best friend knowing I'd just gotten my pussy slobbed on and dug out by her man. I was horrible, but I wasn't that fucked up.

"Oh, come on big red don't be like that." Brooklyn smiled. "It's still early and I'm hungry as fuck. All that work I just put in, I feel like I deserve a meal." He smirked and hugged LaNoir tighter. Here he was being a total asshole and yet I was jealous of her position.

"Shit, I know I could eat again. Where are we going?" LaNoir patted her belly. I agreed to go reluctantly even though I knew I was making a huge mistake. I sat uncomfortably across from LaNoir as we gobbled our food down. The guys chopped it up about their performance while LaNoir rambled on and on about a variety of random ghetto topics in which I had no interest in whatsoever, but I nodded and inserted a 'damn for real' or a 'stop playing' when I thought she needed reassurance that I was listening. I wanted to leave, take a shower and dream all night about Brooklyn dipping his huge dick in and out of my pussy. I could feel him looking at me in my peripheral and I tried my best to not look in his direction.

"So, look I was wondering what's up with graduation? I'm tryna take a bomb-ass trip somewhere to celebrate. We deserve it and I think this should be a couple's thing ya dig?" LaNoir addressed the table.

"Sadie so are you and my boy official or what?" Brooklyn was really trying me with a question like that.

"Officially what?" I mumbled and took a sip of my sweet tea without looking in Brooklyn's direction.

"Bitch are you and Reggie an item like me and my boo?" LaNoir rubbed Brooklyn's hand as she spoke. He grabbed her hand, planting a kiss on it which made my stomach turn. *This mutha fucka really knows how to play a role,* I thought to myself. *Fuck it if he thinks this shit is a game then fine, I'll play right along.* I placed my glass on the table as I slid closer to Reggie.

"So, is that what you want?" I asked in my most seductive tone, leaning into his personal space. Any closer and we would've kissed. Reggie immediately loved the sudden change in my disposition and pounced on the developing opportunity.

"Shit yeah Sadie, stop acting like you don't know I'm into you girl," he cooed. "I need you to go ahead and make this official so I can stop sniffing around you like a little puppy dog," he continued.

"I think you, and me sound really good together." I winked as I continued to entertain the role it seemed everyone wanted me to play.

"Well shit, if you're feeling that good why don't you go ahead and show that man what he's been missing," Brooklyn coerced. I shot daggers out of my eyes in his direction.

"Ha! You know damn well Sadie's snooty-booty-ass ain't about that life!" LaNoir tried me.

Bitch if you only knew how about that life I really am, I thought to myself.

"Nah, y'all chill we have plenty of time for all of that. Sadie is special she doesn't have to do anything extra," Reggie defended.

"Fuck is that supposed to mean? Ain't nothing wrong with doing a lil' bit extra to make your man happy." LaNoir snarled, putting her hand in Brooklyn's lap. LaNoir clearly felt offended even though I knew Reggie's comment had nothing to do with her. I wondered if she would've been rubbing Brooklyn's dick right now if she knew it was just inside of me less than forty-five minutes ago. "I keep my man happy, so he won't have to go sniffing at the next chick's panties." she rolled her eyes as she unzipped his pants and slid her hand inside, stroking his log.

"Damn right." Brooklyn licked his lips as he looked me dead in my eyes. I saw this type of shit turned him on; hiding in public. Well, I'd turn him on high if that's the type of shit he was into. I'd make him want me even more and forget all about LaNoir's ashy fingers. I grabbed Reggie's hand and slid it under my skirt. I wasn't about to let Brooklyn think I was uncomfortable or let LaNoir have satisfaction in thinking she was the only one that could get a little kinky freaky at the table.

"Sadie what are you doing? You don't have to do this," Reggie insisted but never moved his hand from my pussy lips.

"Chill and enjoy that woman," Brooklyn said in a low tone. He was clearly becoming aroused and wanted to enjoy the show. I now see why LaNoir chose the booth in the back corner of the restaurant. She wasted no time in retrieving her man's dick out of his Santa suit. She glanced around, scanning the room quickly before leaning over, taking all of him into her mouth. I couldn't believe he was going to let her suck him off right here at the table knowing I had my fresh juice all over him. I might not have been shit for fuckin' that nigga, but Brooklyn was despicable. The sad part about it was I kind of liked it.

Reggie was so happy to finally get his hands on Yoni that he didn't even notice his best friend biting his bottom lip, staring me down as he got head. Brooklyn was undressing me with his eyes and imagining me on his dick. "Let's get out of here," I whispered in Reggie's ear. I was definitely foul for fucking Brooklyn, that I wouldn't deny, but I wouldn't be double dirty by allowing him to mentally fuck me in front Reggie and LaNoir. Reggie sat up, pulled a few bills from his wallet and placed it on the table as we left LaNoir with a mouth full of Brooklyn's stiff dick at the table.

CHAPTER 4

$\mathcal{M}$ad Maxx and Lady Sadie, those were our club names. Everyone knew D.T.A. as Mad Maxx and B-Boy, but now there were the women of D.T.A; Lady Sadie and Lucky LaNoir. After the night of the Christmas party, we were inseparable, and as much as I hated to admit it, I'd grown to love Reggie. I loved how attentive he was to my needs and he was always a perfect gentleman. Selfishly, I still fantasized about Brooklyn on a regular basis. I couldn't help but to. Reggie was so sweet and gentle, but I craved a savage. Brooklyn was every bit of a beast and he didn't give a shit who knew. I wanted that type of aggression between my thighs. Hell, I'd even envisioned him stroking me during one of me and Reggie's nights of passion, almost calling out his name out when I finally climaxed. I felt guilty every time my mind would drift; I honestly did. The problem was that guilt didn't mean shit when Brooklyn would come around looking like sex on a platter. I wanted him to soak my biscuit with his gravy. My lust for him was building again and I wasn't as strong-willed as I thought I would be when it came to what Yoni wanted. When Yoni called, I let her have whatever she was craving, and I knew sooner rather than later she'd be screaming for Brooklyn's affection. It had been months since our secret meeting in the closet occurred and even with Reggie treating me like a queen, it didn't stop my hunger. Our graduation-vacation was approaching fast, and I made a mental note that I would have Brooklyn inside me again by any means necessary.

"Woo-hoo! We made it!" LaNoir screamed as she threw her graduation cap into the air as we rode down the highway. We were on our way to Virginia Beach in the candy red, 1970's Chevelle with black racing stripes down the center that Reggie's parents bought him as a graduation gift. Reggie had his Ray-Bans on looking like the happiest man in the world as he tightly gripped the steering wheel. Brooklyn and LaNoir were in the back seat and even though I couldn't get him off my mind, it became comfortable to be around Brooklyn without feeling guilty. "I'm ready to hit the water!" LaNoir exclaimed as we walked into her suite. The guys were still outside unloading the car, slowly bringing in the suitcases.

"I'm hungry, that was a long ride." I walked over to the sliding glass door and stepped out onto the balcony. The warmth of the sun felt good beaming on my skin. "Shit girl, I hope Reggie got us a room with a balcony too," I admitted. I'd ran to the restroom as soon as we hit the hotel lobby, so I didn't retrieve a key. I just followed LaNoir to her room, awaiting the guys.

"So, I overheard Maxx telling B-Boy he has something special planned for you," LaNoir gushed. LaNoir couldn't hold water even if she owned a pool.

"Something like what?" I polled.

"Shit, I dunno. They got all hush mouth when they realized I was eavesdropping," she claimed.

"Hmm, I wonder what it could be. I did tell him I wanted some

gold hoop earrings I'd seen when we were at the mall the other day. Maybe it's that." I concluded, shrugging it off.

"Watch this." LaNoir pointed to a group of guys walking down below. "Hey!" she screamed, waving her hands to capture their attention.

"Girl what are you doing? You don't even know them," I interjected.

"Well they are about to know me." She chuckled as she lifted her sky blue mid-drift shirt along with her bra, letting her plump, light chocolate titties swing freely. The guys stopped in their tracks as they watched the show from below.

"Them some nice ti-tays!" one of the guys yelled.

"Let me suck them nipples!" another barked.

"You too green shirt!" the only shirtless one shouted and pointed to me.

"Oh, shit!" I blushed and shot off inside the room. "Girl get your tail in here!" I shrieked. LaNoir jiggled her tits back and forth before returning inside, giggling the entire time.

"Girl you better drop that goody-two-shoe shit and enjoy your vacation! *Tuh-huh!*" She smacked her lips.

"I'm not acting. I'm not down with all that extra shit like you," I rolled my eyes.

"Yeah, okay whatever Sadie. All this extra shit keeps my man from fuckin' extra bitches," she said as she rolled her eyes and flipped her twenty-six inches of Peruvian strands.

"So, you think all that nasty shit Brooklyn has you doing keeps him from sliding his dick into other females?" I tested the water even though I knew it was full of sharks.

"B-Boy doesn't even blink at other bitches without my approval. That's why our relationship works. All the freak shit we do, we do together. We don't have secrets boo," she curled her lip as she spoke, proving I'd hit a nerve. I knew I should have just let the conversation go but I couldn't. LaNoir's cocky disposition was irritating.

"You're telling me without a doubt, that you know Brooklyn has been one hundred percent faithful to you? He has never, ever, not once, planted his stalk where it shouldn't have been," I quizzed and waited for her reaction.

"What don't you understand?" She rolled her neck. "What did I say? He has never and would never because I got that shit on lock." LaNoir snarled flopping down on the bed. "Maybe you should go and see what room you and Maxx are going to be in and stop worrying about who my man is sexing."

"Look I wasn't trying to get your feathers fluffy. I just think men will be men and giving the right place, combined with the right person, a man will only be as faithful as the closet he creeps in." I smirked.

"Bitch what?" LaNoir stood in defense just as the guys walked into the room.

"What y'all pretty young thangs doing in here? Ready to hit the strip? Reggie asked as he wrapped his arms around me, kissing me on the neck.

"What's wrong with you? You okay?" Brooklyn asked LaNoir as he pulled the rest of their luggage inside.

"Yeah, I'm cool Daddy." LaNoir's mood switched instantly when Brooklyn came in. She really was an actress when it came to him. Whatever he wanted her to be she gladly conformed to stoke his ego in that moment.

"I need to change into something more comfortable then we can go," I told Reggie.

"Yeah you do that," LaNoir mumbled. Brooklyn could tell something was off, but he decided to let it go.

"Aye, we're gonna go freshen up then I'll hit you in a bit and see if y'all ready, cool?" Reggie dapped Brooklyn up and took my hand leading me to our lover's suite.

"Reggie! Are you serious? You didn't have to do this!" I gushed in excitement. The room was completely gorgeous, decked in all white. It was a split-level suite with the bathroom directly to the right as soon as you entered with a super-sized jacuzzi to the left. There was a Tufted Button Chesterfield-Style sofa sitting across from the Grecian bed that had white, silk linen hanging from the pillars, and a solid wall of glass that had a perfect view overlooking the ocean waves.

"Only the best for my baby, *mmwah!*" Reggie pulled me close, kissing me on my forehead.

"But this must have cost a fortune!" I melted in his arms. I'd never stayed in a room as elaborate as this. My family vacations were nice, but nothing in comparison to this fully loaded room we'd be staying in for the week.

"I can admit my parents helped. When I told them that I was bringing you here, they were more than happy to assist."

"All for graduation? Plus, your car, sheesh."

"Yeah, my parents are cool and I'm an only child, so you know how that goes... but enough about them. I need you to change so we can hit the strip. I want to get some fried clams, I'm starving." Reggie released me from his grasp, so I could get dressed. I switched out of my ripped denim jeans and designer tee into a long, boysenberry summer dress that flowed when the wind caught it just right. I loved how it cascaded down my back just enough to be sexy without exposing my mini love handles. Reggie texted Brooklyn and we agreed to meet in the lobby. Minutes later we were walking on the strip. Reggie paid for everything I glanced at twice. "Whatever you want Sadie. I promise to give you the world someday," he whispered in my ear after handing me my bag from a local vendor.

We ended up having dinner at Waterman's Surfside Grill after playing a few video games at an arcade; their food was amazing and even LaNoir's mood seemed to have lightened up by the time the check arrived.

"So, what's up y'all tryna take a dip before we head back?" Brooklyn suggested.

"Nah, you're supposed to wait to go into the water or you'll cramp up," Reggie said as he grabbed his to-go box.

"I swear y'all so damn dry," LaNoir complained.

"Literally or figuratively?" I joked.

"Both bitch," LaNoir snapped.

"Whatever LaNoir. We are in a new place, so I guess it wouldn't be a normal outing if you didn't show your ass in public," I shot back.

"Literally or figuratively?" she sassed, using my own words against me.

"Both bitch," I said with a straight face and pointed to her hand. It didn't take a scientist to see she was groping Brooklyn under the table.

"Damn are y'all okay?" Reggie addressed the obvious tension that was brewing.

"I'm good, just tired of her calling me dry because I don't want to have a dick in my mouth in every restaurant we dine in. I'd actually like a meal I can swallow." My top lip curled in disgust.

"Oh, trust I can swallow. But you wouldn't know about that with your dry-ass throat." LaNoir wasn't backing down. She pushed her glass towards me. "Have a sip."

"Ladies, chill. It's not even that serious. We are supposed to be here celebrating our graduation, amongst other things, so y'all need to dead all that petty beef shit." Brooklyn moved LaNoir's hand and got up from the table.

"Yeah, what's the problem? We are supposed to be having a good time," Reggie added.

"I'm good love. I'm just ready to hit the water," LaNoir spoke softly as she grabbed her handbag and headed towards the exit.

"Babe these next few days are all about us okay? Just focus on us and I'll make you the happiest woman in the world alright?" Reggie was correct. This weekend was about our accomplishments and nothing more. I decided to do as he'd suggested and kept all my attention on us... and Brooklyn. It wasn't long before the four of us were feeling the warm salt water between our toes. LaNoir as usual wasted no time stripping down to her neon orange two-piece thong bikini, jumping into the waves. *Maybe you were just being a bitch,* I thought to myself as I sat in the sand, stretching my legs. I enjoyed the water splash around my calves as I watched Brooklyn in my peripheral, sure not to let Reggie catch my drifting eyes. I was lost daydreaming about the Christmas party when I heard Reggie calling my name.

"Sadie? Sa-dieee? Are you okay?"

"Yeah," I laughed lightly, realizing I'd been in a zone.

"Ready to head back?" He extended his right arm and helped me to my feet.

"Where're the freaks of the week?" I did a quick scan of the beach, but I didn't see Brooklyn and LaNoir anywhere.

"They left a few minutes ago; something about LaNoir's swim top breaking. I dunno." he shrugged. "We agreed to link up later for drinks. Is that cool with you?" he asked.

I wish Brooklyn would take a sip from my cup, I thought to myself. "Yeah that's what's up." I smiled hard at Reggie and he pulled me close.

"That's what I've been missing. I need to see that smile more often," he stated then kissed me softly on the lips. He was always so gentle with me. It was like I was a porcelain doll and he was scared I would break if he handled me too roughly, but that's what I craved. I wanted him to be rough with me. Pull my hair, smack my ass, fuck me in a closet at the spare of the moment. I tried to stay focused on us, but it was hard when everything I wanted was the opposite of that Reggie was providing sexually. We headed back to the hotel hand-in-hand. I wanted to be happy with Reggie, I really did, but he wasn't the one making me expose my pearly whites. Thoughts of Brooklyn were lingering in my mind and I basked in the thought of fucking him again. I wasn't sure how I was going to do it, but I decided right then that I was going to have him lapping at my juices before this trip was over.

CHAPTER 5

"*I* need to talk to the hotel manager about of the staff," Reggie said as we walked into the lobby. "I specifically asked for a freshly stocked bar, and with the money I'm spending, it shouldn't have been an issue. You should check out the gift shop; see if you can find something for our parents," he suggested.

"*Mmkay*," I agreed and walked over to see what treasures the swanky little shop held. I found a beautiful glass sculpture of a dolphin jumping out of the ocean and thought it would be perfect to add to my dad's collection seeing that he loved the sea creature so much. I grabbed one for Reggie's mother as well then stood in line to check out. I looked out the window towards the front desk and saw Reggie talking to the hotel manager. Right then Brooklyn exited the elevator with LaNoir nowhere in sight. He stopped and exchanged a few words with Reggie then walked in my direction after Reggie pointed me out. Butterflies filled my stomach as he strolled over. I loved watching him walk, it was like he had to make room for that pole that hung between his thighs.

"What you got there beautiful?" He reached out to see the statues I held. His words sent shivers down my spine. "Nice," he said as he retrieved them from my hand, placing both on the check-out counter.

"That will be eighteen ninety-seven," the cashier announced as she started to wrap the gifts.

"Here you go and keep the change." Brooklyn handed her a twenty-dollar bill and grabbed the bag.

"Where's Reggie?" I asked when I noticed he was no longer standing at the front desk.

"Off complaining about the room or some shit. But don't worry about that. What's up with you though? Why are you and LaNoir going at each other? We are supposed to be here as friends and I'm getting a little nervous. Anything you want to get off your chest?" He didn't look at me as he spoke. His eyes stayed locked on the elevator door. He selected the button for my suite and didn't even blink in my direction. *Bing!* The doors opened, and a small family exited before we stepped inside.

"It's nothing. I'm good," I said uneasily. I was slightly nervous being around Brooklyn alone and this elevator ride wasn't helping my slutty thoughts. I wanted him in the worst way and this would probably be the only chance I'd get to have him to myself.

"Are you sure about that? I mean we can do our own thing and keep our distance if need be, ya dig?" He finally cut a glance at me and we locked eyes. I knew what he meant; he wanted to make sure I wasn't going to say something we'd both regret later.

"I'm cool Brooklyn I promise." I allowed a little smile to creep onto my lips even though it was a complete lie. I wasn't cool. I wanted to lift my dress and set my hot pussy all over his lips. I wanted LaNoir to disappear altogether and I wanted to be the one flopping my fat ass up and down on his dick.

"See that's what I like right there. That smile is dangerous." He touched my cheek.

"How dangerous?" I egged him on. He knew exactly were my thoughts had drifted and I was tired of hiding it.

"Sadie, you don't want these problems," he said with conviction, staring me down.

"I don't want problems, you're right. I want you." As soon as those words left my lips I pressed the emergency stop button on the wall. In two steps I was in his arms and he didn't push me away. We began kissing passionately, caressing each other like starving animals. I wanted him, and it was now apparent that he felt the same.

"Sadie wait there's something I need to tell you." He paused, pushing me away, and tried to get me to calm down, but I wasn't in the mood for regrets.

"Right now, Brooklyn! Right now's all that we have. You can waste it or play with it." I lifted my dress, exposing my hairless, naked pussy. I never wore panties under a summer dress; I needed to let Yoni breathe. His eyes widen as he saw my juice box waiting for his touch. He hesitated before dropping to his knees, stuffing his sexy face in between my thick thighs. He had no trouble suckling at my clit as I leaned against the elevator wall. "Oh yes, baby yes!" I moaned as my nectar began to flow. *Bam!* He slammed me into the wall mercilessly, lifting me up as he loaded all of his manhood into my throbbing hole. I locked my legs choking his waist with my arms secured around his neck. *Bam, bam, bam, bam!* He beat my pussy unapologetically. I wanted him and he wanted me, and we gave in to our desires. "Fuck me, Brooklyn!"

"Oh, I'm fucking this pussy, Sadie. I'm fucking this sweet pussy!" He stroked me hard, fast and deep. I shook as I began to cum. "Oh, Sadie! It's coming Sadie! It's coming!" he whispered in my ear repeatedly as he bit it softly. He pulled out and spilled his seeds unto the elevator floor. We stood in silence, looking at each other for a few seconds breathing like stallions after a horse race before we started adjusting our clothes and mentally preparing to go back into reality. I pressed the number ten and the elevator resumed motion. "Sadie listen, there's something I need to tell you." Brooklyn's face turned sour and he looked as if he'd just heard the worst news of his life. His face read grief as the doors of the elevator sprang open.

"Whatever it is we can talk about it later." I didn't want to brush him off, but I didn't want to risk anyone seeing us together.

"No, I really need to talk to you now! It's important." He grabbed my hand, but I yanked it away.

"Brooklyn, what are you doing?" I whispered. "I promise we can talk about it later. I need to take a shower before Reggie comes back," I insisted and walked towards my room. Brooklyn followed me like I was a fox and he the hound.

"Sadie please just wait!" he begged but that didn't stop me from pulling out my key card and unlocking the door.

"Get the fuck on Brooklyn before you get us caught up!" I spat before opening the door and walking inside.

"Surprise!" My ears rang, and the unified voices echoed down the hall causing my heart to sink when I saw my suite filled with my friends and family. Everyone was dressed in all white and even Reggie had changed his clothes to mirror the crowd. He stood in the center of the room waiting for me to come further inside.

"Oh shit! What is all of this! Why are you all here?" I was confused and overwhelmed. *Why the fuck is my family here?* I thought as I inched my way forward. I heard some music begin to play as I got further into the room Reggie began to sing 'When I First Saw You' by Jaime Foxx. "When I first saw you, I said, 'Oh my.' I said, oh my, that's a dream, that's my dream..."

I instantly felt dirty and disgusted with myself. This man was beyond good to me, hell who am I kidding he was the best boyfriend I'd ever had, and I'd just fucked his best friend on the elevator... again. He didn't deserve that, but I was selfish and greedy with lust. I glanced around the room and spotted Brooklyn in the corner with LaNoir by his side. He looked away from me and I could tell he was disappointed with himself too. He knew Reggie was going to propose yet he fucked me anyway.

When Reggie finished the song, he took a knee retrieving a small black box from his pocket, grasping my left hand. "Sadie, I've loved you since the day we met, but I never knew it until now. You've become my best friend and I trust you with my life. Please do me the honor of being my lover, as well my friend, forever. Sadie Marie Tennan, will you marry me?" Tears welled in my eyes, but not because of Reggie's proposal. I'd just gotten fucked like a cheap whore minutes ago and now I'm being asked to marry Reggie in front of all our friends and family. There was no way I could tell him no with all these people around and watching. I'd already violated him without his knowledge I couldn't dare humiliate him by saying no. So, I did what everyone expected me to do.

"Yes! Yes, I will!" I screamed as tears ran down my cheeks. He placed the beautiful princess cut diamond ring on my finger and gave me the warmest embrace. He lifted me up and swung me around causing me to catch a glimpse of Brooklyn. LaNoir was glaring hard as fuck. I could see Brooklyn was extremely uncomfortable and trying to mask his guilt. Everyone erupted with praise, clapping and yelling, "Congratulations!" as we walked around the room, showing off the glorious gem that now decorated my hand. Reggie came from money; his mother was a therapist with multiple best-selling, self-help books under her belt and his father had his own business working for multi-million dollar corporations as a financial advisor. They were white collar, overly ambitious types and paid out of their asses. I'm positive they were responsible for the hefty rock that adorned my finger. I knew people with money, but these were the first people of color I knew that had wealth. Reggie never worked a day in his privileged life and being the only child, they spoiled him excessively. He always obtained whatever he wanted so I'm sure they were like putty in his hands when he told them that he wanted to propose.

CHAPTER 6

"Well I'm not one for long engagements so I think we should start planning right away," Mrs. Montana suggested after kissing my cheek. "Reggie mentioned that you loved winter so why not have a Christmas themed wedding?" she suggested.

"Mariam let the girl enjoy her engagement party! It hasn't even been twenty-four hours yet and you're already asserting yourself into her life. You'll have plenty of time to tell your ideas to her later. Let the kids enjoy themselves," Mr. Montana scolded.

"Thank you, Sir." I smiled as he gave me a hug.

"Welcome to the family, Sadie! Call me Dad!" he added. "We'll have to make arrangements to fly your father and brother out for a family dinner soon." I smiled and nodded at his suggestion.

"I'm so proud of you baby girl!" My father gave me the tightest hug when I finally found him in the crowded room. He was never overly affectionate with me or the coddling type, so it was a slightly awkward embrace.

"Thanks Dad, but why are you proud? I didn't do anything."

"You got that rich mutha fuckah to put a ring on it," my obnoxious brother Gabriel commented while stacking his plate full of the gourmet food Miriam had catered for the event.

"Stop. Just stop. Damn I haven't even had the ring on my finger for thirty dang-on minutes and you're already clockin' my pocketbook." I sighed.

"Watch your damn mouth. Just because you have that sidity bastard glued to your loose-ass pussy lips don't mean shit to me," Gabriel grumbled.

"What the heck? Damn Gabe it's my freakin' engagement party and this is the stuff you wanna pull!"

"Now calm down! Everybody just calm down! Gabe show your sister more respect than that! You act like you were never raised. Sadie baby you know you have to overlook ya brother. He ain't been right since... well since ya momma passed. Now we ain't come here to make you upset on your special day. I know I wasn't much of a father to you, but I did the best that I could. A man's not supposed to raise a girl by himself. They never turn out right... but not you. You turned out just perfect Sadie baby. You did well for ya self and from the looks of it you're gonna be doing even better."

I rolled my eyes at Gabe and he grinned before he began shoveling food into his filthy mouth. He enjoyed aggravating my soul and did so every chance he got, but Daddy was right; Gabe was never the same after Mommy passed and the fact that Daddy used most of the insurance money to send me to college didn't sit well with him either. As the eldest he figured he should have gotten the lion share of what was left over after the funeral expenses but ended up with a few hundred instead. Sensing my discomfort Reggie pulled away from his parents to check on me.

"Mr. Tennan, how are you sir? Gabriel." Reggie extended his hand. Gabriel looked at his hand but continued stuffing his face.

"Hey Reggie, or should I say son?" My dad grabbed his hand and gave a shaky laugh.

"Definitely son. Your beautiful daughter just made me the happiest man on the planet." He smiled and wrapped his arms around me.

"I can tell. By the looks of that ring you spent a whole lot to make sure she said yes, huh? How much that set you back?" Gabe chimed in.

"Oh my gosh! What the hell is wrong with you? Reggie ignore his rude and tasteless ass," I instructed.

"Well, nothing but the best for my baby. She deserves it," Reggie responded. Daddy nudged Gabe and shot him a 'you better chill the fuck out' look. "Well if you can excuse us I have a few more people I want to introduce to my wife-to-be. Oh, and my parents would like to fly y'all out soon for a family dinner." Reggie escorted me off and I was grateful that he did.

"Thank you," I whispered.

"I'll always be here to save you, remember that." He kissed me on my hand. "Now let's show off that ring!" He laughed. I hoped that, that would have been the last horribly awkward moment, but it wasn't. After being introduced to a few of Reggie's family members I found myself at the bar playing over the day's events.

"You look like you need something stronger than that weak-ass mimosa," LaNoir said as she approached.

"I'm dry like that remember." I rolled my eyes and turned, facing the bar.

"Look bitch I can keep this up all week or we can let this petty shit go and turn up." She stared waiting for a response.

"What are you staring at?" I questioned. LaNoir could hold a grudge longer than Niki Ménage's braids so I was surprised by her suggested change of heart.

"I figured you must have a lot you're dealing with especially being paraded around as some trophy with that big-ass stain on your dress." She pointed down at my dress and she was right. I had a big white spot on my dress and I knew exactly where it had come from. I immediately grabbed one on the linen napkins and dabbed it in a glass of ice water that was on the bar.

"That ain't gonna come out with water." LaNoir took a sip from her glass.

"Shut up, LaNoir," I hissed.

"Ladies now that the older people have started to leave let's turn up Aggie style!" Reggie announced as he walked over with Brooklyn following. "What did you spill on your dress baby?"

"Nothing. I got it, it's okay." I tried to rub even harder, but it seemed to just spread the cum stain around even more.

"You want me to help?" Reggie tried to grab the napkin, but I yanked away.

"No! I just... I just... I just need to change clothes!" I blurted, causing a few of our friends to look in our direction.

"I think Monica used club soda," LaNoir commented.

"Monica?" Reggie looked up.

"Monica Lewinski," LaNoir laughed hard and loud and Brooklyn grabbed her by the arm.

"Look clearly she's had too much to drink so I think we're just gonna call it a night and turn in. Y'all should be sharing this moment together anyway. We can turn up with y'all tomorrow, cool?" Brooklyn dapped Reggie up and gave me a head nod. I knew he was uncomfortable as well, so this was the perfect excuse to leave and I'm glad he didn't waste it.

"Tell that hoe to take a shower Reggie," LaNoir mumbled before Brooklyn pushed her out the door.

"What was that about?" Reggie questioned. "I thought y'all would have squashed that petty shit by now."

"You know how LaNoir gets when she drinks."

"Yeah, yeah you're right," he agreed. "We'll tonight is all about me and you. I want you to go take a shower and put on something sexy for me while I get the rest of these people out of here, okay? Tonight, I want to have you all to myself." Reggie smiled, and I felt sick to my stomach. As much as I wished that things had unfolded differently tonight, I didn't regret having passionate, hot sex with Brooklyn in that elevator and that was the problem. I loved Reggie, but I was in lust with Brooklyn.

I snuck off to our bedroom as Reggie began wrapping the party up. I turned the shower on full blast as I tried to wash my sins away. "What the fuck is wrong with you?" I said aloud as the scalding water landed on my delicate skin. I began crying as I thought about what I was doing. I felt like I was becoming my mother in so many ways, all the bad ones. She and Daddy married right after high school. She was the love of his life, but he wasn't hers. She had gotten knocked up by Franklin Greene the star football player at Lincoln High and he wasn't about to drop his college plans to take care of a kid he never wanted by my mother. He left with no regrets and no forwarding information. His family wouldn't even acknowledge Gabriel when he was born and my dad, Kevin, was there to mend her broken heart and provide for her as well as Gabe. He loved our mother unconditionally and you would have thought that she wouldn't even blink an eye in Franklin's direction after years of having no contact with her or even trying to have a relationship with Gabe, but no. Those feelings still remained. After all those years she still ran to him when she heard he was back in town. They had an ongoing affair for about two years before anyone became aware and the way it was revealed was the worst. She was shot by Franklin's wife. She'd suspected him of cheating and when she walked in on them in their home she lost it. My mother was shot in her back as she tried to run out of the house naked. Franklin didn't even come to the funeral or try to contact Gabriel. He told the reporters all kinds of bullshit to make himself look like he was the real victim. He was a real piece of shit and I think that's what influenced my brother's bitter actions. He developed a hard shell and totally dismissed his feelings about everything. Seemed like every time someone tried to get close to him he found a reason to cut them off without warning. We were close before mom's passing and I could talk to him about everything, but now we were like strangers.

"Babe." Reggie startled me as he stepped into the shower. "Why is the water so damn hot and what's wrong?" He hurried to turn the heat down when he saw my face. It was clear that I was upset, and I hated that he'd noticed. I thought I'd have more time to get my emotions in check before he came into the room.

"Oh, it's nothing. I'll be okay." I tried brushing him off, but I knew he wasn't going to let it go.

"Sadie, I need you to let me in. You're going to be my wife and I have to know that I'm doing everything possible to make your life easier." He wiped my cheek with his thumb.

"I was just thinking about my mother and how I wish she was here to see this. It's going to be hard to plan a whole wedding without her."

"I'm sorry babe. I know it's not the same, but my mom will be more than happy to step in and help relieve the stress of planning a wedding. We can even add a nice memorial in her honor at the ceremony."

"Why are you so good to me?" I looked up into his eyes.

"Because you deserve it."

"I don't. I'm a horrible person."

"Why would you say that about yourself?

"Reggie listen, there's something I need to tell you."

"Sadie, stop. I'm not perfect either. Whatever you feel you need to say right now don't. Please don't. Don't kill my dreams of us being together. Whatever happened before you said yes no longer matters. This is our chance for a new start."

"But there is something you really need to know"—

"Sadie please. Don't ruin what could be a perfect memory. I love you Lady Sadie and that will never change. Nothing can change that." I looked into his eyes and I could tell he wanted to live this fantasy and that's what it was… a fantasy. If he'd known, I'd fucked his best friend twice we wouldn't be in this shower having a heart to heart right now no matter how much love he proclaimed to have.

CHAPTER 7

The drive home was mainly in silence; I blamed it on mental exhaustion when Reggie noticed my quiet disposition. The months passed by quickly... almost too quickly. LaNoir and I stopped the personal jabs, but we didn't have much to say to each other after the beach trip. We were soros, so we had to be in each other's space from time to time and Reggie was none the wiser. He still did a few shows here and there with Brooklyn, but I made sure to keep my distance. Brooklyn and I continued to hide in public whenever we were forced to be in the presence of the other, making sure we didn't do or say anything that would suggest anything other than friendship. Even after all the drama my thighs still clenched when he entered the room.

Eventually Reggie stopped doing music altogether. He was determined to follow in his father's footsteps by joining his financial guidance group and Reggie Sr. couldn't have been prouder. He groomed his son to be just like him and it was working. Christmas came even faster, I agreed with Mrs. Montana that a holiday-themed wedding would be perfect. I was spared no expense when it came to décor; Miriam instructed me to pick whatever I wanted, and she gladly paid the tab. With a Winter Wonderland theme there were crystals and glitter covering everything the eye could see. It resembled a Disney on Ice production; how everything came together was beyond beautiful.

"It's almost time," my coordinator sang as she popped her head in the room. "Can I get everyone except for the bride to line up outside?" Everyone began to leave the room and I found myself alone with only my thoughts and that wasn't a good thing.

Well, you have no choice now. You have to go through with it, Sadie. My thoughts became louder and louder as the room fell silent. *You can do this. Reggie is a good man and he has given you the world. You love Reggie.* I reassured myself. Knock, knock, knock! I was slightly startled by the taps on the door. I lifted my gown, so it wouldn't drag as I walked over to see who was there.

"Sadie," was all a familiar voice was able to mutter.

What the fuck is he doing here? My adrenaline began to rush. I cracked the door open and saw Brooklyn's back facing the door. "What are you doing here? Shouldn't you be helping the Groom get ready since you are the best man?" I spat. He turned, and our eyes connected.

"Yeah, I *uh*—I'm here because of him. He asked me to give this to you." He had a small box in his hands. I opened the door fully then he placed the small light blue package on my palm. I pried it open and it contained the red nose he wore at the Christmas party last year. There was also a note attached that read: *The night we became one.* I looked at the words and guilt consumed me. That was the night we'd became a couple officially, the night that I couldn't stop thinking about, but it had nothing to do with Reggie. It was the night Brooklyn and I shared in the closet. I still wore the scarf I'd taken as a reminder of it.

"Why did you bring me this shit!" I shouted and threw the box at Brooklyn's chest.

"I didn't know what it was!" Brooklyn stepped in the room and closed the door behind him. "He just handed it to me and said that it was important that you got it. How was I supposed to tell him no? I would have given it to one of the bride's maids but everyone's headed over to the courtyard." He lowered his head. "Look I'm not trying to cause you any pain. I wish we could take back that night and the time in the elevator, but it is what it is. It happened and it's over with. You're with Reggie and I'm with LaNoir and that's how it's supposed to be."

"You're right, that is how it's supposed to be." I turned my back to him, so he couldn't see the tears forming in my eyes, but the giant mirror hanging in front of me blew my cover. We stood in silence staring at one another for what seemed like forever.

"Then why can't I stop thinking about you?" Brooklyn's voice was shaky and full of emotion. I turned around and was met with his full lips on mine. We shared an undeniable passion as he cuffed my face kissing me with such a force I almost lost my balance. He lifted my gown, pulled my white lace panties to the side and forced his fingers into my pussy.

"What are you doing? We can't! We can't!" I squalled, pushing him with the weakest force ever. My mouth said those words, but my body screamed 'yes!' The truth was I didn't want him to stop touching me. I didn't want him to remove his hands or take his lips from mine. I wanted him to rip this elaborate and over-priced gown off of my tingling frame, plunge his thick, long sword into me and fuck me like we were in Medieval times. He was raw with Excalibur stiff between his legs ready for war but this couldn't happen, not now or ever again. At least it shouldn't have. Brooklyn pulled his dick out and stuffed my tight walls as he lifted me on the dresser. He'd only gotten about three pumps in before we heard a knock on the door and the knob turning. He jumped back, pushed his dick back inside his black pants and began adjusting the rest of his attire.

"Sadie, it's show time," Nikki, the wedding coordinator said as she walked into the room.

I pulled my gown down quickly and blurted, "Close the fuckin' door!" The look on her face revealed she knew exactly what she'd walked in on and she stepped back out and closed the door just as fast as she had entered.

"Fuck!" Brooklyn grunted.

"We can't do this anymore," I whispered as I pushed past him and exited the room.

"Are you ready?" the coordinator asked uneasily? I nodded.

"Are you sure?"

I cleared my throat and swallowed my mistakes. "Yes, I'm ready," I confirmed. "And by the way, you didn't see anything."

"For what you're paying just call me Stevie Wonder," she said as she helped me fix my dress back to perfection. "You know there's no shame in changing your mind. Rather it be now than ten years later."

"I said I'm ready," I snapped. I knew she wasn't the cause of my frustration, but I was so agitated at this point.

"Well let's go make you an honest woman then," she said as she led me to the courtyard. I was going to marry Reggie 'Mad Maxx' Montana and that was that even if my pussy belonged to Brooklyn.

CHAPTER 8

"*L*ife goes on," is what my mother would say whenever I'd get into trouble. I missed having those kinds of conversations with her. She wasn't a big disciplinarian; seemed like she always had a witty phrase to justify all her un-ladylike actions. I wish she was here to help me get through my troubles, but technically she never got through her own.

After the wedding, our interaction with Brooklyn and LaNoir became few and far in between. When Reggie would suggest couple activities, I'd mysteriously fall ill or conveniently have a prior engagement. They showed face for major events like our first-year anniversary, but eventually our friendship faded. I wasn't surprised when LaNoir called to announced that she and Brooklyn had eloped two years later. They were spontaneous like that, so it only seemed fitting for them to run off and get married on a whelm.

When I agreed to sit with Brooklyn, I knew the danger it held. He sent me a message via Facebook and I eagerly responded. I hoped after all the time that elapsed that he was just a temporary craving and that I wouldn't want to act on my emotions even though I thought about him often. I loved Reggie...I really did...but I lusted Brooklyn.

"Lady Sadie. Wow it's been a long time." Brooklyn looked relieved as he sat across from me.

"Brooklyn 'B-Boy' Thompson, yes it has. How's LaNoir?" I asked even though the slut in me could care less.

"LaNoir is LaNoir." He sighed. "That's actually why I needed to talk to you. We've been going through some problems and unfortunately, they involve you."

"Involve me how?" *Oh my gosh, she found out? When? How? It's been years!* I thought as a million ideas flooded my mind. I didn't want my past transgressions to reach Reggie.

"Listen, what I'm about to say is gonna be a hard pill to swallow." He sighed again. "LaNoir has known about us from day one, Sadie. I know this is shocking and maybe even devastating, but it's time for the truth to be out... all of it." Brooklyn's words sent a cold chill throughout my body.

"What's going on? I'm confused?"

"I just need you to listen and think before you react, okay?"

"I'm listening." I raised my eyebrow and awaited his revelation.

"LaNoir has known about me and you from the very beginning. She was always hanging around after our performances and the first time you came with her I approached her about getting your number. I asked her a few questions and you know how she is; she flipped the conversation and made it about herself. She basically told me I wasn't your type and started telling me how she and I would be a better fit. She seemed like she was really into ya boy, you know? After a few dates she said that you thought Maxx was kinda fly and gave me your number to pass to him."

"Wait, what? Hold on that wasn't true at all and I never wanted Reggie. Hell, I didn't even pay him no real attention until you came around." I sat up in disbelief.

"Sadie, just listen. I know all of that now, but I didn't at the time. I just need you to listen. So, like I was saying, LaNoir basically hooked you and Maxx up to get my mind off you because she knew deep down, with you was where I wanted to be. I really wanted to get with you and that drove her insane. I'm not saying I was right. Fuck I was wrong as hell for how I'd throw you up in her face. I'd say lil' rude shit to her when we'd have an argument or any time she felt like I was giving you too much attention. So, she started coming at me with some extra freaky sex shit to divert my mind back to her and I'd fall for it every time."

"So, she knew that we liked each other is what you're saying? What does any of that have to do with me now? Does she know that we fucked in the closet or in the elevator? Please don't tell me she knows about my wedding day!" I twisted my lips awaiting his response.

"The night of the Christmas party you had on that sexy-ass, red lace elf costume that drove me insane; LaNoir as well. She saw how I looked at you, lusted for you and she let that-- we let that cloud our judgment."

"Cloud your judgment. What does that even mean?"

"She offered me something I couldn't turn down... she offered me you."

"What the fuck are you talking about Brooklyn? What do you mean she offered me to you!" I demanded.

"She said that she would let me have one night with you if I promised to never do it again." He exhaled. "And I agreed."

"Wait, I'm still confused. You're saying she was the one who set up the closet shit at the Christmas party?" I was baffled.

"Yes," he sighed. "She gave me your number and told me what to text. I needed you to wear that scarf because I didn't want you to see..." his words trailed off.

"See what Brooklyn?" I questioned.

"To see this." He pulled out his phone and handed it to me. "She told me I could have sex with you, but at the last minute she changed her mind."

I took the phone from his hand and pressed play, so I could view the video that was on the screen. There it was, a video of me bent over in the closet with that plaid scarf tied around my eyes. The same damn scarf I had around my neck right now. The video was dark, but you could still make out everything that was happening because the flashlight was on. The camera zoomed in on my pussy as small fingers begin to rub on my lips and my clit. I knew that hand! It was LaNoir's; she had a tattoo of a smiley face on her middle finger. Next LaNoir's face appeared in the frame and she started sucking on Yoni. She'd ate my pussy from the back while Brooklyn recorded everything. As he zoomed out I can hear him talking and I can see her gripping an extra thick, black strap-on. She stands then inserts the fake dick into me and started fucking me from behind. I guess that explains why the rhythm was off.

I couldn't even watch the rest. I threw the phone at him and stood up.

"Sadie, wait! I'm sorry. I know this is a lot to find out right now, but I need you to know everything!" he pleaded.

"What else is there? You just showed me a video of you and my best friend violating me!" I shouted and saw the waitress look in my direction.

"Sadie, I know and I'm sorry. There is so much more you need to know… about Reggie," he blurted and waited to see how I'd reply to his statement.

"What about Reggie? He has nothing to do with this bullshit y'all made me apart of!" I needed answers and I needed them now.

"Sit down, please!" He looked around and we were quickly gaining unwanted attention. I sat but spoke harshly.

"Look I don't know what kind of sick game you and LaNoir had or have going on, but you keep Reggie out of it! I made some mistakes, I'll admit that, but Reggie is a good man and I don't want him hurt because of me!" I cried. Brooklyn pulled out a photo from his wallet.

"Sadie this is my son, Nathaniel." He placed the photo on the table and slid it over slowly. I picked up the photo and saw an all too familiar face looking back at me. Nathaniel was the spitting image of my two boys.

"What are you trying to tell me, Brooklyn?" I mumbled as tears rolled from my eyes. Pain sunk into my heart as my chest began to tighten.

"Do you want me to say it? I think it's completely obvious. Reggie is Nathaniel's father." Brooklyn's words left me in total shock and disbelief.

Fuck this! I thought, grabbing my purse and coat. I rushed out of the coffee shop, fumbling with my keys as I desperately tried to unlock my door.

"Sadie wait. We need to figure this out! I need to tell you everything!" Brooklyn yelled as he grabbed my arm.

"Get the fuck away from me Brooklyn! Don't you ever fuckin' touch me again!" I opened my car door and hopped inside. I sped out of the desolate parking lot like I was at a KKK rally. My heart was pounding, and I could feel the adrenaline spreading rapidly from head to toe. I felt like I had tunnel vision; I couldn't focus on anything but the dreadful secrets that came from Brooklyn's mouth and I didn't want to deal with it. Not now, not ever. Suddenly his full lips and light eyes didn't seem so damn tantalizing.

Tap, tap, tap! "Are you okay? Mrs. Montana?" Mercedes, our babysitter was trying to get my attention, but I was completely zoned out. I didn't even remember arriving home. Reggie and I lived in a beautiful gated community called Brent Wood Estates; we'd gotten our five thousand square foot home as a wedding present from Reggie's parents. His mother insisted in helping me design each and every room. We even had the nursery completed two years before the twins, Josiah and Chandler was born.

"Poor people plan, rich people do," Reggie's mother would say every time I'd tell her my plans for the house. Miriam was sweet but had her ways. I knew she only wanted the best for Reggie and I, but she'd often overstepped her boundaries; especially after the twins were born. She inserted herself as a mother figure that I never asked her to be. Sometimes she became unbearable and I'd have to ask Reggie to speak with her about boundaries.

"Hey Mercedes, what are you doing out here?" I managed to mumble. The cool air nipped at my nose when I rolled the window down.

"The boys were outside playing in the leaves. I'd just told them it was time to go inside when we saw you pulling in super-fast. Is everything okay?" I could see the concern in her eyes. "No offense, but you parked kinda crazy," she noted as she took a step back pointing at my horrific parking skills. At this point I didn't give two rat turds about anything, let alone how I'd parked. All I could do was paint a fake smile to keep the tears from falling even more.

"I'm fine, just exhausted. I had an extremely tiring day. Thank you for watching the boys while I ran my errands." I forged a grin.

"No problem," she said as she moved out of the way so I could get out of my silver Benz. "Chandler has a scrape on his hand. Him and Josiah were doing a bit of roughhousing, but he's fine," she mentioned and closed the car door behind me.

"Okay. Hey listen, do you think you can give the boys their baths tonight and get them ready for bed? I'm a bit worn out and need to focus on a few things before I hit the sheets myself."

"Sure, I don't mind. I promised them I'd read them a book before I left anyway. I can make it their bedtime story." She smiled. Mercedes was our Pastor's daughter and a true blessing when it came to assisting with the twins. I'd be lost if it wasn't for her stepping in on countless occasions. I'd hoped to utilize my degree in accounting, but there was no way I could compete with the big dogs that held the accounts of my new circle of peers Mariam practically pushed into my life. I'd always been receptive of other's needs, so I went in another direction by starting a personal assistant business. I'd originally hired Mercedes as a favor to the Pastor and First Lady Viller after they'd mentioned having a few issues with her behavior. I figured I could be a mentor as well as provide a positive outlet for the young chocolate beauty, but once I saw how well the boys interacted with her, I decided to hire her as a nanny instead.

"Mommy!" the twins screamed in delight as I entered my home.

"Hello my Ju-ju beans!" I managed a frail smile for my babies and I immediately thought about the picture of Brooklyn's son Nathaniel. He looked so much like my boys they could have been triplets.

"Mommy are you okay?" Josiah asked. He was very intuitive and always knew when I was in a bad mood even though he was only five years old. Chandler was more of a daddy's boy. He mimicked everything Reggie did.

"I'm fine Ju-ju bean. I want you and your brother to take a bath and get ready for bed. Mercedes is going to read you a bedtime story, *mmkay?*" I kissed them both on top of their curly heads and watched them rush up the stairs with Mercedes following. I headed right into Reggie's office. If there were any truth to Brooklyn's story it would be in his office. He was so well organized I was almost afraid to touch anything in fear of him noticing that I'd been snooping. I'd never gone through his things before. Shit I never had a reason to. He was so predictable and perfectly posed for the world, I always knew where he was at every moment of the day. At least I thought I did until now. *There is no way Reggie could have fathered a baby outside or our marriage, and definitely not with LaNoir's ratchet as,* I thought as I began searching through multiple drawers. "I don't give a fuck how much that lil' bastard looks like my sons," I hissed under my breath as I began to become a little more frantic with my search. If Reggie really fathered another son, I wasn't going to rest until I found undeniable proof.

CHAPTER 9

*B*eep! Beep! Beep! I groaned as I rolled over in my California King. *Why the fuck did I drink that entire bottle of champagne?* I thought as my right eye crept open and was met with immediate pain from the throbbing headache that formed instantly. "Fuck you, Dom Perignon," I moaned and rolled onto my back. I'd spent hours carefully searching through Reggie's office for anything that would link him to LaNoir and her son, but to no avail I'd found absolutely nothing. I laid there in the same clothes I'd worn the night before and used the corner of my tan Frette One Bourdon sheets to wipe the drool that had escaped my dry lips. I didn't need a mirror to know that I looked just like I felt- like shit. I imagined a troll under a bridge looking like a beauty queen in comparison to myself at that moment. I managed to pull myself from my overly soft mattress, stumbled into the bathroom and splashed some cool water on my face. Red-eyed with dark circles, I looked like a raccoon that had been smoking ganja all day. I turned on the shower, disrobed, then sat on the toilet to release my stretched bladder when I thought, *What the hell Sadie? How are you going to get through this?* I pulled my aching body into the steamy hot shower and let the water run over my head, completely saturating my hair. I wanted to scrub away the pain that was still fresh, but I knew that wouldn't work.

One thing was for sure; I was certainly glad it was the weekend because I would not be able to function under these circumstances. I needed to think long and carefully about my next move. I needed to be slicker than a snake slithering on ice. If Brooklyn brought this to my attention, then clearly LaNoir knew he was coming to meet with me, but does Reggie know that I'm aware of his little bastard seed? I debated calling him once I'd finished showering and slipping into my robe but decided against it. I needed hardcore facts before everything was laid out on the table. This was some life-altering shit that I wasn't prepared for. I pulled my hair into a high ballerina ball and dabbed a little concealer under my eyes. I needed some cucumbers to reduce the slight swelling that lingered, but I'd just have to make due for now.

Tap, tap, tap. "Mrs. Montana you have a phone call," Grace, the housekeeper called out.

"You may enter," I said loudly. The door crept open and she scurried over handing me the house phone.

"It's Mr. Montana," she whispered before exiting the room and closing the new Marbella Wrought doors I had installed last week.

"Thank you, Grace." I sighed. If I'd known, it was Reggie on the other end I would have told her to give him some kind of excuse. I didn't want anything to do with his child-producing-ass right now, but I guess I had no choice.

"*Mm-hmm.*" I cleared my throat. "Hello."

"Sadie! How's my favorite daughter in law?" Reggie's father, Reggie Sr. sang happily in my ear.

"Oh, hello," I was surprised and let out a huge sigh of relief.

"Well you sound disappointed dear. Were you expecting someone else?" he replied.

"I'm sorry I thought you were your son. How's the trip going?"

"You know how these business trips go. You spend all of your time trying to persuade these people that you know what's best for their business, but they are determined to make you go over the details page by page line by line for hours just to come to the same conclusion you summarized on page one." He laughed. "How's my grandba-bies?" I hesitated with my response because I hadn't seen Josiah and Chandler all morning.

"They're um, they're fine. Chandler has a scrape on his hand, boys being boys..." my words faded.

"Oh no. Well tell my future little businessmen that Paw-paw has something special for them when I get back."

"I sure will and when will that be exactly?" I pried. I knew these business trips had unreliable time frames. Dealing with multiple corporations kept Reggie and his father traveling all over the states, even internationally on occasions. The best thing Reggie could have done was to follow in his father's footsteps. The name Montana carried a lot of weight around here. Hell, Reggie's parent's estate made damn near two of ours. I even lived in the east wing for a few weeks after the twins were born. Miriam insisted on being near her grands and she could be a mighty force of wind when she was determined to have her way. Josiah and Chandler had the best of everything, she made sure of that. She'd wanted more children of her own, but complications during her delivery made Reggie the sole heir to the Montana's fortune.

"Well, they should be closing negotiations within the next few days. The paperwork is drawn, but you know they have to go through everything with a fine-tooth comb," he explained.

"Yes, I understand."

"I just wanted to check on you and the boys. I'll tell Reggie to give you a call when he gets out of his last meeting today," he added.

"No, it's okay. I'll give him a call later because I'm going to meet with a potential client myself," I lied.

"On a Saturday?" he inquired.

"Yes, it's just a brief sit down to go over what services I offer, nothing major."

"Understood. I'll see you all soon then. Goodbye." He ended the call and she tossed the phone on to the bed. I was super relieved it wasn't Reggie on the other end. I needed more time to see how I was going to proceed. I hurried to get dressed and glanced at myself in the mirror as I headed towards the door. The black leather pants and cream blouse I'd paired with it did my figure justice. Even though I'd gained weight carrying the boys, my thick frame was still dripping with desire. After the night I had, I was determined to be well poised and keep up appearances. No one needed know anything about my family unless I released it. I learned that from Miriam years ago. She definitely made sure her family's name steered clear from any public shame.

I used my cell phone to search for information about our old friends. *That's it, they just want money,* I thought to myself. According to Facebook, Brooklyn and LaNoir had decent jobs and lived in a nice neighborhood; nothing in comparison to our home, though. Reggie delighted in having upscale living quarters and consistently spoke of upgrading which I didn't see why we'd need more space than we already had. I didn't want any more children even though he constantly hinted at having a baby girl. To be honest this home was a bit much to manage by myself and if it wasn't for the housekeepers I would definitely struggle with its upkeep. Sadly, money was the only reason I could think of that made sense. Why else would Brooklyn wait so long to bring up Reggie being the biological father if it was indeed true. Two and two wasn't equating to four but somehow, someway, the truth would have to come out. I just wanted to be ahead of it all, so I wouldn't be punched in the face by any more shocking details. The way I felt at the coffee shop yesterday was enough for me.

"Mommy!" I heard Chandler say as I entered the kitchen.

"Good morning, Ju-ju." I smiled as I leaned over to kiss his curl-covered head. "Where's your brother?"

"He's in the dining room eating."

"Well shouldn't you be at the table too?"

"I was helping Ms. Grace put the dishes away," he chimed.

"Is that so?" I shot a displeasing look at Grace as she wiped the cabinets down. I'd told her on several occasions not to allow the boys to assist her with her house duties. My boys would never have to wash a dish in their life if I could help it. "Well how about you go find some fun kid stuff to do and leave the chores to Ms. Grace

52

okay?" I smiled slightly to assure him that I wasn't upset. As he ran off and I decided against reprimanding Grace for disregarding my wishes. I had more than enough on my plate right now to be concerned with what the maids were doing. "Tell Mercedes to take the boys to the park today. I'll be home by dinner," I instructed. Grace nodded in agreeance. With my Tina Firenze handbag under my arm I headed out the door. I had some heavy detective work to do if I wanted to have all the facts in order before I confronted Reggie.

"Good day Mrs. Montana," George the security officer at my husband's office greeted when I strolled up to the front of the building.

"Good day George. How's Tina and the kids doing?" I smiled and batted my eyes lightly. I had to lay the charm on thick if I wanted to get in and out with no questions.

"They are well, thanks for asking. What are you doing up here on a Saturday Mrs. Montana? The office is closed ma'am," he said politely.

"Being a great wife." I laughed. "Reggie left some important papers in his office and asked me to retrieve them. I have to send them to him immediately, so he'll stop calling my phone," I lied.

"Well allow me to escort you to his office." He held the door open so I could pass. We made small talk on the elevator as we traveled to the fifth floor. Bing! The door opened, and I stepped off as George followed. As we approached Reggie's office I had to think fast because I knew it was locked and I didn't have a key. I began to search through my bag acting like I'd misplaced it.

"Well... it seems I have left the key at home. George can you be a dear and open his office for me?"

"I'm not authorized to do that ma'am. I can only open Mr. Montana's office in the event of an emergency."

"Well doesn't this look like an emergency to you? Here I am trying to get some very important papers for my husband, your boss, asked me to get for him, and you're telling me that you can't let me in."

"Ma'am I do understand that, but we have very heavy rules we must follow, and I'm not authorized to let you into his office."

"I see. On the elevator you mentioned George Jr. was applying to several colleges correct?"

"Yes, ma'am but"—

Well I'm sure a letter of recommendation would go very far to help secure his spot. Wouldn't you agree?"

"Well yes ma'am it would but"—

"Then let's get this door unlocked okay?" I patted him on his arm and smiled. He was reluctant, but he pulled the keys out of his pocket and unlocked Reggie's office.

"See it wasn't that hard now was it? That will be all I can find what I need on my own thank you."

"Ma'am I"—

"I said that will be all." I gave him a stern look that let him know I was not to be fucked with at this point. George was a great worker and I meant him no harm, but I wasn't about to let him, or anyone deter me from my goal. I set my bag down on top of his desk and took a seat on his oversized leather chair. I began searching through his drawers. I was confident that there was something that would link him to LaNoir's little bastard but again I found nothing. I was becoming frustrated and about to leave when I thought about Angeliek. Angeliek was Reggie's secretary. She was down to earth and professional but knew how and when to have a good time. She would low-key drop the dime on new interns who thought they could cozy up to the boss to move up the corporate ladder. I trusted her, and I even gave her special gifts on holidays to thank her for her input.

I made sure to straighten his chair before going straight to Angeliek's desk. I did have access to her computer. I'd watched Angeliek type in that login probably over a hundred times to give me personal information about these amateur leeches in their church choir heels. I logged into the computer and in less than five minutes I had Reggie's schedule for the last three months sent to my personal email. I felt a slight sense of relief even though I had no real evidence in my grasp yet.

"Find everything you needed?" George asked as I strolled past. I saw the look on his face when he realized I wasn't carrying any papers.

"No, he must have placed them somewhere else, but I appreciate your services. You can expect that letter for George Jr. in a few days." I kept my composure and walked to my vehicle. I glanced at him in my rearview as I sped off. I knew he wouldn't say shit if he wanted to keep his job, so I wasn't worried. I still didn't have of a single shred of evidence to tie Reggie to that kid Brooklyn claimed was his and I was becoming more pissed by the minute.

CHAPTER 10

$\mathcal{I}$ drove to my office to further my research. I knew that was the only place I could go to have the privacy I needed in order to put this puzzle together. I searched through both Brooklyn's and LaNoir's Facebook profiles again just in case I missed something the first time I played detective. LaNoir's most recent post was from a few days ago in reference to going to see a Dr. Zebono at The Mayo Clinic in Archdale. I quickly googled the facility to get the address and was surprised to see it was a treatment center. They would be closed today so I made a mental note to go first thing Monday morning.

'I'm That Chick' by Kelly Rowland crept out from my pocketbook which meant someone was calling. *Please don't let it be Reggie,* I silently begged the most-high. I looked at my phone and my heart started dribbling double time. It was him. As bad as I wanted to scream obscenities into the phone I knew I had to keep my composure. I took a deep breath and put a fake smile in my tone as I answered.

"Well hello husband," I said cheerfully.

"Hello beauty. Father told me he checked in with you and the boys. I assume everything went well at the office today?"

I choked. *Fuck! He knows!* I thought. That damn George had to have called as soon as I left. I tried to play off my shock. "What do you mean love?"

"Father said you had to meet with some potential clients today. I assume they signed with you, yes?"

"Oh." A huge sense of relief rushed through my body. "I'm actually preparing for their arrival as we speak. They should be here any minute now," I lied.

"Well I know you will show them your worth. I won't hold you. Kiss the boys for me," he replied.

Great he bought it, I thought. "When can we expect you love?" I needed to know how much time I had before he came home. Unlike most men Reggie was extremely observant of my whereabouts. He'd inherited that trait from his mother. Miriam was obsessed with time management and seemed to always keep track of every move Reggie Sr. made, at least from my perception. I remember when Reggie and I became engaged; he refused to let me go anywhere alone for three whole months. At first, I thought it was cute and thoughtful, but then it became annoying and I needed my space. I didn't understand how KeKe Wyatt did it. That insecure obsessive shit almost drove me insane.

"No later than Thursday. I'm hoping for Wednesday, but you know how meticulous these people can be."

"Understood. See you soon my love." I sweetened my tone even more. I wouldn't have been surprised if he had sugar pouring from his ear the way I laid it on. I had less than a week to piece this shit together and I was determined to find out every last detail even if I had to go to LaNoir myself.

Tap, tap, tap! I snapped out of my hypnotic trance when I heard someone knocking on the glass door. I walked out of my office and my stomach hit my feet when I saw who was standing there. I unlocked the door and cracked it open. "Why are you here?" I asked dryly.

"We need to talk." Brooklyn pulled off his Ray-Bans and I could see the lightness in his eyes that use to drive me wild.

"About what exactly? You said what you had to say," I snapped.

"Sadie, I know you're upset, but I need to talk to you."

"There's nothing left for us to talk about. What do you want, money? How much do you need to make this go away?"

"Make this go away? This is a child! My son! You can't just sweep him under the rug!" he barked.

"Your son? I thought you said he was Reggie's?"

"You're being petty. He is MY son regardless of how he came to be, he belongs to me. I am his father and there is nothing I wouldn't do for him, that's why I'm here."

"So why did you come to me? Why didn't you just go directly to Reggie?" I polled.

"Reggie knows he's the father. He knew from day one. As soon as LaNoir found out she went to him and told him, but he tried talking her into an abortion and we don't believe in that."

"Oh now y'all have morals and shit? Where were your morals and values when it came to videotaping me in the closet!" I spat.

"That was years ago and though I'm not proud of it now. I did it, I allowed it, I participated, and I own it. I'm asking you to forgive me and don't let this come between you helping my son. He is innocent and has nothing to do with this."

"What kind of help could you possibly need from me? If you don't want money, then why the fuck are you here?" I rolled my eyes while crossing my arms.

"Nathaniel, my son... he's sick. He has AML and it looks like he's going to need a bone marrow transplant." He lowered his eyes, but I could see sorrow spreading across his face.

"Leukemia." I wasn't expecting him to say that at all. My mind skipped back to the appointment I saw on LaNoir's page. As mad as I was at this whole situation I now understood why he was here. If my child was fighting for his life I'd do anything to make sure they had the best chance at survival too. "Damn Brooklyn I'm sorry. Look come in my office, so we can sort this out." I lead, and he followed. I took a seat at my desk and sighed heavily at the thought of having a child in that type of condition.

"I know it's a lot to take in and I'm sorry. I really am, but I don't know what else to do. LaNoir tried contacting Reggie but all we get is voicemails. She even went to his office but was escorted out before she even hit the elevator. I tried waiting on him after hours but there was no way I was getting close to him with all the security he has at that building. We aren't looking for hush money. Hell, you would have never heard from us if Nathaniel didn't get sick, but the reality is he is, and we need more information about his genetic history to see if he does need this transplant. Reggie could be a possible match."

"Reggie a possible match?" I repeated.

"Yes. Do you think he'd be willing to takes some test and see?" I looked in Brooklyn's eyes and I could see this wasn't a game. This wasn't some ploy to milk money from us. This child, his child, was ill and needed help. I might have been a bitch, a cheater and a horrible friend, but I wasn't a monster, and as much as I dreaded having to confront Reggie, it was something I knew had to be done sooner rather than later. I assured Brooklyn that I'd talk to Reggie as soon as he set foot into our home. He still had business to take care of so there was no point in pouring oil into the water unless I planned on shaking shit up. I told Brooklyn he'd hear from us soon and meant it. I locked the door after we left my office and headed home.

I was surprised to see Miriam standing in my living room talking to what looked like a Backstreet Boy when I walked in. His clothing style was so elaborate I wasn't sure if he was a decorator or a pop star in the making.

"Miriam what are you doing here?" I questioned.

"Well I tried calling but I couldn't make out anything that maid of yours was saying. You really should think about hiring some American help if they are going to be answering your phones dear," she insulted.

"Grace speaks English Miriam."

"Grace speaks English with an accent. Get her some classes or something." Miriam was always complaining about something that was going on in my home and it was starting to annoy me.

"And who do we have here?" I addressed the highly tailored white man standing in my living room with a clipboard. His platinum blonde highlights were almost blinding.

"This is Ferlando Jez'Terrio. I flew him in to finally get this living room in order," she gushed.

"I decorated the living room myself. It was the only room aside from my bedroom I did without your help."

"I know dear and that's why he's here. That reminds me. We need to go have a look at the master suite. Those colonial valance and panels sets have got to go." She laughed her fake rich people laugh and Mr. NSync joined in.

"No, I think you need to go." I was now pissed. I was already stressed to the max and didn't need Miriam to add to it. I needed time to get my thoughts in order.

"I beg your pardon?" Miriam clutched her pearls, literally.

"Miriam, I mean no disrespect, but I have a lot on my mind right now and I don't need any other distractions."

"What could be so disparaging that you'd talk to your mother like that?"

"You are not my mother." My tone changed from annoyed to disgusted and I knew she felt the temperature in the room drop.

"You're right. I apologize. I meant no harm by my statement. You are the daughter I never had Sadie, and I just wanted to surprise little Reggie with something nice when he came home."

"I appreciate your interest, but I'm happy with MY home. Mr. Jessorro, Jetslorro or whatever you name is, I hate you had to come all this way just to have your time wasted, but I will not be needing your services. Please see your way out.

"Well wait one second. He came a long way to fix this... this ... well I don't know what to call it."

"You too, Miriam." I rolled my eyes and stormed off into the kitchen. Only a few seconds passed before my mother-in-law continued to crowd my personal space. I motioned for the house-keepers to exit.

"I dare you act that way in front of a guest. He has been published in Lovelle magazine for goodness sake!" she squalled. Recognizing her heightened disposition, she lowered her voice and gained control of her emotions. "All I'm saying is that you could have talked to me after he'd taken his notes for the house."

"I could have talked to you? About my house? What is it that you're not understanding? I didn't ask him to come. You could have asked me before you had this stranger in my home. Jesus, Miriam you didn't even ask if I wanted to redecorate. You just inserted yourself as usual."

"Well if that's how you feel, why am I even here?"

I could tell I hit a nerve. "You're here because you invited yourself over. I'm not saying you're not welcomed here. I'm just asking for a little more respect when it comes to the decisions in my home."

"Your home? You wouldn't even have this home if it wasn't for me. I saw that cheap three-bedroom house on the east side you wanted Reggie Jr. to buy. What a disgrace. Imagine my grandbabies growing up in that shack of a home, in that neighborhood," she insulted.

"Miriam what are we doing? How did we get here? I really need to have my focus elsewhere. I'm not trying to do this with you right now."

"I was born here, you married in." She was in full force. The sweet mother-in-law I met years ago was nowhere to be found. She'd been replaced with at mega beast and was rearing her ugly head.

"You're right. I married into this seemingly picture-perfect family. I moved into this fancy house filled with overpriced décor that I didn't even pick out myself. I even let you decide how my children's rooms would be decorated all to keep your precious little Reggie happy, and for what?"

"Someone sounds a bit ungrateful. I mean if I'd come from a mediocre past with a whore of a mother and a disabled father I'd be overjoyed to marry into a family like this. I won't even mention all the unsavory details I found out about that thug of a brother you have." Miriam's words cut deeper than any knife could. I knew she was a force to be reckoned with for those that crossed her, but I didn't know she was a level five hurricane. Her words could do more damage than Katrina.

"I told you that stuff in confidence, not for you to throw it back up in my face because I will no longer fold to your demands."

"You didn't tell me anything I didn't already know. Do you honestly think I didn't have you checked out before my son proposed to you?" she confessed.

"Had me checked out?" I was surprised. Was she admitting to stalking my life?

"Yes Sadie, I had you checked out and I told my son not to propose to you if you want to know the honest truth. Unfortunately, Reggie is as stubborn as his father and wouldn't listen to me. So instead of protesting I decided to try to make the best of the situation. I took you under my wing and groomed you to be the daughter I never had. I introduced you to the elite life and this is the thanks I get. He should have left you where he found you." She bolted out of the kitchen, out the front door and into the driveway. "Shoot I forgot I had the driver drop me off." She pulled out her cell phone and called her car service.

"You think your family is so perfect, don't you!" I yelled as I followed her outside. "Your perfect house, your perfect cars, your perfect image. It's all bullshit! Reality check Miriam- everything the Montana's touch isn't gold! Did you know your precious Reggie has another child?" I blurted. I knew I shouldn't have let that escape my lips before having the chance to address my husband, but I was fed up with her shit. She needed to know that her perfect little fairytale life wasn't so fuckin' perfect. I searched her face for shock, but it never came. I waited for her to call me a liar, but the words never left her mouth. That's when it hit me. She knew. Miriam knew that Reggie had fathered LaNoir's child and never said a word.

"Dear sweet Sadie, there is nothing about this family that I don't already know about. It's about time you caught up." She said nothing else as her car pulled into the driveway. I stood there feeling like a total fool and she didn't even blink in my direction. I didn't wait to see her drive off. I stormed into the house and ordered all of the staff to leave the premises.

CHAPTER 11

*M*ercedes came downstairs and found me tearing apart Reggie's office. I wasn't looking for anything I was hurt and just wanted him to know how much.

"Mrs. Montana what's going on? I heard you yelling outside and put a movie on for the boys, so they couldn't hear the commotion. Is everything alright?" she asked.

"Clearly everything isn't alright!" I cried. Mercedes was silent not knowing how to respond. "I'm sorry. I didn't mean to take my anger out on you." I walked over to her and gave her a hug. "Thank you for taking care of the boys. I don't know where I'd be without you." Tears wouldn't stop flowing from my eyes. "Oh, gosh! Look at me I'm a mess." I caught a glimpse of myself in the mirror.

"You are an amazing woman Mrs. Montana and a great mother. Let's go upstairs and I'll help you get into bed," she offered.

"I'll be fine. Can you just make sure the boys are okay?"

"Josiah and Chandler are good, I promise. Let me help you... please?" I saw the softness in her eyes and it gave me peace. I grabbed a bottle of the good stuff as we walked by the bar. I cracked it open and guzzled damn near half the bottle before went reached the top of the spiraled staircase. I took a long bath while Mercedes tended to the twins then I slipped into my robe and climbed into bed. Tap, tap, tap. Mercedes peeked her head in.

"I was just coming to check on you," she spoke softly.

"Thank you. I'm alright," I lied.

"Are you really?" she said as she took a seat on the bed.

"I will be."

"Now that sounds like an honest answer. Let me take that from you." She pulled the empty bottle of liquor from my hand. I was feeling the effects in full force at this point. Mercedes instructed me to roll over, so she could pull the sheets down and I obeyed. As she pulled the soft linens up to my neck my robe opened up slightly exposing my breasts.

"Oh, shit I'm sorry," I apologized and pulled my robe together.

"Sorry for what? We are both women."

"Sorry for everything. I'm your employer. You shouldn't have to see me under these conditions."

"You think you're the first family I worked for that had issues? We all have issues Mrs. Montana." Mercedes retrieved the rosehip oil from my nightstand, squirted some into her hand and began rubbing my arm.

"You don't have to do that," I spoke.

"I know, but I want to." She massaged the oil into my hand and arm working her way up to my elbow. She squirted a bit more into her hand the placed it on my chest.

"Wait what are you doing?"

"I'm helping you relax."

"No, not like this you can't do that," I protested.

"Why not? No one's here but us. You sent the staff home remember and the boys are in the bed."

"No, this isn't' right."

"Why isn't it? It feels good doesn't it?" She slid her moist hand over my breast in a circular motion. Rubbing the oil into my soft skin. I grabbed her wrist.

"No this isn't right you have to stop. You have to leave."

"But I don't want to. Mrs. Montana I'm not a child. Regardless of whatever my parents have told you I'm nineteen years old and I'm not immature like these other girls around here." She used her free had to pry my fingers from around her wrist. "Let me help you get some rest." She took the oil and squirted it directly onto my chest this time. She opened my robe and began gliding her hands gently over my exposed breasts. I had to admit it did feel good. I closed my eyes and allowed her to caress me. She took her time and covered every inch of my breasts and stomach. She began lightly rolling my nipples between her fingers and I couldn't help but to moan in pleasure.

"See, doesn't that feel good."

"Mercedes, wait"—

"*Shhh*, relax," she whispered in my ear before taking my nipple into her mouth. I was ashamed to admit that it felt more than good. The way she flicked her tongue over my hard nipples made me cream between my thighs. She licked her way down to my navel and before I had a chance to protest any further she'd stuck her face between my legs and Yoni was delighted. Mercedes ate my pussy better than anyone I'd ever been with and I enjoyed every minute of it. I'd never been with a woman before, and least not willingly. LaNoir had violated me and the thought of it began to turn my stomach. I'm sure the liquor I'd consumed contributed to that as well seeing that I hadn't eaten anything all day. I was a nervous wreck on the inside and it was going to come out in the form of vomit. I shoved Mercedes face away from my soaked pussy and barely made it off the bed before vomit spewed out of my throat like a volcano. It splattered across the floor the stench of liquor mixed with stomach acid filled the room.

"Oh my God! I'm sorry! I'm so sorry!"

"It's okay." Mercedes wiped her mouth with the back of her hand then ran off to the bathroom to retrieve a towel. She covered the hot mess on the floor and looked for a bag to place it in after scooping most of it into the expensive cloth.

"Don't worry about it. That's what the maids are for. Grace! Grace!" I called out.

"Mrs. Montana you sent everyone home… remember?"

"What? Well why the hell did I do that? I'm not cleaning this shit up!" I regurgitated more of the smelly sauce.

"Oh gosh! We're going to have to get you to the restroom." Mercedes grabbed me by the waist and helped me to the toilet. After about twenty more minutes of praying to the porcelain God I managed to make it to my feet. Mercedes cleaned up the mess I'd made and was coming up the stairs with a glass of v8 juice.

"I heard it was good for hangovers," she said as she handed me the glass.

"I can't take the smell in here. I'm going to sleep in one of the guest rooms tonight." I waddled my way to the closest guest room and climbed into bed.

"Mrs. Montana," was the last thing I heard Mercedes say before closing my eyes.

CHAPTER 12

"Wake up!" The sound of Miriam's voice dug into my soul. I couldn't believe she was standing over me looking like the grim reaper.

"What are you doing here? What are you doing in my room?" I said angrily as I pulled the covers close to my body.

"You're in the guest room and I'm helping you get yourself together before my son gets home." She yanked the curtains back and the sunlight pierced my eyes.

"I don't need you to help me with a damn thing. Now get out of my house, Miriam."

"I'm taking you to breakfast so we can get your head together. I figured something had to have happened to trigger your absurd outburst yesterday. We must discuss how you are going to present yourself when Reggie Jr. arrives. He's going to be highly upset when he hears how you treated me."

"How I treated you?" I sat up in the bed in disbelief. *She must be out of her rabbit-ass mind,* I thought.

"You threw me out on into the street like I was a hoodlum! Not to mention the scene you caused with my guest. You embarrassed me to the high heavens. You should be thanking me for persuading him to come back next month. I had to do some heavy bargaining and that doesn't come cheap." She folded her arms.

"You really are out of your damn mind," I mumbled.

"Oh, I'm a lot of things, but I assure you I'm the reason the Montana name gets things accomplished in this city. I am the glue that keeps things from falling apart, unlike yourself. One little infidelity and you act like your whole world has come to an end. Pathetic. You better grow some tougher skin if you even plan to make it when Reggie returns. Here it is almost past noon and you're still in the bed." She yanked the comforter off the bed. "Go clean yourself up and meet me downstairs. We have to get things in order and fast," she demanded before stomping out of the room.

"This bitch must want me to go to jail." I tried replaying the events that led to me waking up in the guest room, but everything after kicking Miriam out was a blur. I pulled myself from the bed into the bathroom and sat on the toilet for what seemed like eternity. I thought about Miriam and wondered how long she'd know about Nathaniel. She'd probably known the very night Reggie slid his meat into that funky bitch LaNoir. I'd done my own research and came up with nothing, so I decided I might as well listen to what my monster-in-law had to say in hopes of finally getting some real answers.

"Well it took you long enough," Miriam complained as I reached the bottom of the stairwell. I was dressed to perfection because I knew how Miriam conducted business. She'd play nice over an overly priced meal then by the time the waiter arrived to ask if we wanted some exotic dessert added to our bill she'd have you in whatever position she wanted you in. Even though this should have been a private matter for me and my husband, she let it be known that she was already a part of the bullshit. This family probably had more bones than all the graveyards in North Carolina combined, but she'd find a way to cover it up or make it work in her favor.

The staff was back, and everything looked as if it had never been touched. "Grace, can you tell Josiah and Chandler to come here please."

"Mercedes took the boys to church ma'am," she informed. Damn it was Sunday. I'd have to make up these past few days by taking them to a movie or toy shopping. I had a brief flashback of Mercedes rubbing my chest last night and then it all came flooding back.

"Damn shame everyone knows where your children are but you." Miriam smacked her lips in disgust.

"Can we just go and get this over with?" I opened the front door and walked out.

"TWO MARTINIS WITH EXTRA OLIVES PLEASE," Miriam told the waitress after being seated at a table in The Saux Restaurant; just one of her many personal investments.

"Keep that second one. I'm not drinking."

"I wasn't for you," Miriam waved the waitress off.

"Can we get this over with. I'm not feeling my best."

"Well that's completely obvious by the look of your hair and face." She pointed. "I'll schedule you an appointment with Rodrigo for tomorrow."

"I didn't agree to come here for you to spew your insults at me. I want to know what you know about this baby," I demanded.

"What you're going to do is lower your tone. I brought you out of the house in hopes that you'd conduct yourself as a lady should and not like that rachet I was introduced to yesterday. Now I realize I said some things that were truly awful and should have never came from my lips and for that a do apologize. After all we can't choose the family we are born into." She paused as the waitress returned with her drinks. "We are humans, and all fall short of the glory. That being said, we are not perfect. My son, your husband is not perfect. He is a man and men will do what men have always done. That straying eye was born into their system. They are just wired that way." She was hard when she spoke. Her face showed no compassion.

"So, it is true; Reggie has another son... with LaNoir," I said as tears poured from my eyes. Miriam threw a napkin in my direction.

"What are you doing? Don't you dare shed a tear for all these people to see. Next thing you know your clients will have your personals spread throughout the city and that's bad for business," she snapped.

"You just confirmed my HUBAND has a whole baby by my best friend!"

"And! You aren't the first wife to have her husband creeping around and reproducing. Hell, in my day men had a whole family on the other side of town. Sometimes in every town they ever lived in. 'Papa was a rolling' stone was inspired by true events. Besides, that girl was nowhere close to being your best friend. Y'all young people go around holding onto labels as if they are supposed to mean something. It didn't mean anything when you were lusting after her man now did it?" She took a sip from her glass as my sadness began to turn into frustration.

There was no way she could have known about me and Brooklyn, I thought. The only way that could have been possible is if LaNoir's wide-mouth-ass had said something to justify her fucking Reggie.

"What the hell are you talking about?" I decided to play dumb. No point in throwing myself under the bus, seeing that I didn't know what she actually knew.

"Oh, don't play coy with me. Even Ray Charles could see that boy had a thing for you and the way you tried avoiding eye contact at the engagement party let me know that you had a thing for him too. I'm glad you just made the right choice by staying faithful to my son. How embarrassing would it have been to have him lose his woman to his best friend. He would have been devastated." She took a bigger sip.

Whew! She didn't know anything about Brooklyn and I. "Brooklyn is happily married to LaNoir. All I need to know is why and how long did Reggie plan to keep this from me?"

"Don't try to tell me anything about Brooklyn and his happiness. I've known that boy most of his life. It's a shame he didn't follow in his parent's footsteps. They are extremely successful while he's over there playing house with a baby that isn't even his with that whore of a wife. He sacrificed his entire inheritance when he married that tramp. His father wasn't about to let that skank run through his hard-earned money and I couldn't agree more. At least with you I didn't have to do much polishing. That girl couldn't even spell class let alone act as if she had some. Reggie doesn't know about Nathaniel and that's the way I want to keep it." Miriam's words rang like a bell in my ear.

What the hell did she mean he didn't know about Nathaniel? The look on my face told her exactly what I was thinking.

"But Brooklyn said"—

"Brooklyn doesn't know shit! I fed LaNoir the lines to tell her husband to prevent him from asking too many questions. I told her word for word what to say and how to say it. I send them a monthly payment to provide for that child and to keep their mouths shut. I even had them sign paperwork to make sure that this doesn't turn into a scandal, but now I see I have to pay them a visit to remind them of the terms of our agreement." She smacked her lips.

This bitch was a monster. A certified demon, I thought. Here I was thinking I was the worst person on the planet for my past, but this boss bitch took the cake, ate it, spit it up and slung it in your eye. She didn't give a damn about anything but her perfectly projected image.

"How could you keep the fact that Reggie has a son from him? He's going to lose his mind when he finds out."

"What are you deaf or just dumb?" She sat up in her chair and pointed that crinkled finger at me. All the facelifts in the world couldn't hide the age her hands shown. "Reggie Jr. is not to find out about any of this."

"He's going to want to know he has a child. He's not the abandoning type."

"You're damn right he's not. He got that from his father. He would bring that little bastard into your home, have him around Chandler and Josiah; is that what you want? You really want her little bastard to share what should be your children's legacy?"

"Miriam even though I'm crushed by the fact that Reggie fathered a son with LaNoir there is no way I'm going to conceal that from him. Reggie's a good man and that baby didn't ask to be here. That child is innocent in all of this," I defended.

"Reggie's a good man! Reggie's a good man!" she mocked in a

whiny voice. Her condescending tone made me want to reach across the table and slap some real sense into her. Miriam was a truly beautiful woman. She reminded me of Lynn Whitfield only brown skin, but this part of her personality made her look like a witch. She was ugly deep down in her core and it was seeping through her pours. "Reggie is a man who couldn't keep his thing in his pants and now I'm paying for this little bastard to keep our family together. Do you want to ruin what you have?" She guzzled the rest of her drink and slammed the glass down on the table causing a few people to look in our direction. Clearly, she was highly irritated and losing her classy demeanor she was so keen on portraying.

"I don't care about what people think. Do you even know that child is fighting for his life? What if Reggie could help?"

"That's just a ploy to get more money from me. She's told me about his so-called illness a few months ago and I offered to have him seen by my doctors and they refused saying they'd already established his visits elsewhere. Ha! What kind of specialist could they afford? They refused to have him seen by my professionals so that only equates to one thing; this is all a bullshit scheme to try to get me to cash out, but they can kiss my ass if they think they're going to get a dime over what I'm currently paying them. Do you know that hussy had the nerve to show up at the office! Thank God I'd already informed security and they are on the banned list. Neither one of them will be able to get within ten feet of my son to ruin his life because of one drunken night." She grabbed the other martini and sucked it down her throat like her mouth was a vacuum. "You will not utter one word to Reggie and that's not a request. I promise you'll hate me even more if you even whisper the name LaNoir to him." She stood, tucking her beige Hermes bag under her arm. "Now get yourself together and that house better be in order by the time they come back from their trip. Find yourself a way home while you're at it," she hissed before walking out of the restaurant. Miriam Montana might have run parts of this city, but one thing was for damn sure; she didn't run me.

CHAPTER 13

"She needs some young meat!" Gabriel's words made me giggle on the inside, but I wouldn't allow him to see me crack a smile. Our relationship hadn't improved over the years. He always shot negativity every chance he could. My father's health was slowly deteriorating, and you'd think that would be enough for Gabe to stop his foolishness. Instead it seemed to fuel his reckless behavior. I'd bailed Gabriel out of jail over twelve times, four was within this year alone. I wanted to practice tough love, but every time I tried to enforce it my father would call on his behalf. He never said thank you for the many times I came to his rescue. He never even tried to at least act like he was trying to get himself together.

I offered to move my father into my home, so I could look after him myself, but he refused saying that he was fine living with Gabe in the home I'd relocated them to. "Daddy, I don't know what to do," I cried as I sat on the foot of his bed. He'd just awakened from a nap when I'd arrived. I'd called our car service and had them take me to the one place I knew I could think freely with no distractions; my father's.

"Now if you're goin' to come in here with all this drama the least you can do is be honest." He sat up in the bed. "Hand me that pillow over there... the big one," he instructed. I grabbed the oversized green and black pillow and placed it behind his back. "Thank you, baby girl. Now you know you have to tell Reggie everything you know. I know it hurts and it's gonna to be hard, but you are his wife and if you want to stay in that marriage you have to tell that man everything; and I do mean everything. You don't want him to find out through the media or from someone else's lips what you knew the whole time do you?"

I sat there with my head down listening.

"Why you let that old bitch punk you?" Gabe said as he brought in a plate of food for my father.

"I didn't let her do shit. That's just how Miriam is. She wanted to keep her picture-perfect lifestyle by any means necessary," I countered.

"That's one mean bitch." Gabe sat the plate of candied yams, deviled eggs, honey baked ham and collard greens on our father's lap. "I'd fuck that old bitch into submission."

"Why do you have to talk like that? Don't you have any respect?" I rolled my eyes as he walked out of the room.

"Fuck you and that old as broad!" he yelled from the kitchen.

"Ignore him Sadie, baby. You know he ain't got it all," Daddy said before blessing his food. "Dear God bless this food and the hands that prepared it. Bless my baby Sadie and guide her as she makes a needed, yet hard, decision. May her family stay strong and heal where they are broken. In Jesus' name, amen."

"Thank you, Daddy. I'm going to get out of here. The boys should be home by now." I stood and placed a kiss on his forehead.

"Bring my babies over here to see me. I got a 'pointment on Thursday with the doctor but I don't think I'mma go."

"And why not? Daddy you have to go. Now I know you're sore and it hurts to move at times, but you have to keep your appointments."

"Aww you hush! That man can't tell me nothing I don't already know. I'm old and I'm dying. That's the order of life. Once a man twice a child. I just ask that I go before I start stinkin' on myself; that ain't no life for a man." He stabbed a piece of ham onto his fork and shoved it into his mouth.

"Well for one you have to stop eating this kind of food. Daddy you have high blood pressure. You're not even supposed to be eating pork."

"You gotta die from something. Let me die happy."

"Daddy"—

"Bye Sadie. Get on outta here girl so I can enjoy my food." He shoved an egg in his mouth and grinned with a little cream on his teeth.

"Bye Daddy." Nothing I said was going to make him replace that plate with something healthier, so I let him live.

"Yo' what's up with that lil' chocolate drop you have working for you?" Gabe asked before I could get out the door.

"Who are you talking about?"

"That fine ass, thick broad who be watchin' my nephews."

"Mercedes?"

"Shit yeah. Lemme get her number."

"Let you get her number? Fuck outta here Gabe. I wouldn't let you near her. She's not like these lil' hoes you drag up in here all times of night. Matter of fact which one of your lil' chicks you got cooking this greasy-ass food you're feeding Daddy because I know it wasn't you. You burn water," I insulted.

"That would be me," a short, curly-headed white girl walked out from the restroom.

"Ain't no way Becky cooking collards," I laughed.

"Sandra, and I'm Italian," she corrected.

"Well nice to meet you Sandra." I turned to walk out the door, but Gabe still wanted answers.

"Wait. I'm serious. Drop ol' girl's math so I can get in that." He placed his hand on the door keeping me from opening it.

"You're a real piece of shit you know that? You don't give a damn, do you? Sarah is right there."

"Sandra. I'm Sandra Dee... like in the movie," she corrected.

"She ain't my bitch. That's one of Bishop's hoes. He sent her over here to work off some money she owes him."

"How is it you have people working for you, but I haven't seen a dime of bail money?"

"I ain't ask you to do shit. And hell, that's the least you can do since you went to college on me," he snapped.

"Get the fuck outta my way Gabriel." I pushed his hand away from the door and left. I wasn't about to spend another minute arguing with his stupid, ungrateful ass. I didn't ask Daddy for a dime of that insurance money, and I'd even purchased the house they were living now, but that wasn't good enough for Gabe. Nothing ever was. Kelly Rowland's vocals crept from my purse as I got into the back of the town car. "Hello," I answered once I saw it was Mercedes.

"Hey Mommy! I hear the twins sing in unison."

"Hey my Ju-ju beans! How was church?"

"It was a-mazing!" Chandler said.

"I'm glad you enjoyed it. I'm on my way home now. Can you give Mercedes the phone baby?"

"Sure mommy." Chandler's little voice filled my heart with love.

"Mrs. Montana, hi. How are you feeling?" Mercedes answered.

"I'm much better than what I was. Thank you for asking and thank you for taking care of the boys for me. I have a lot going on right now, so I appreciate you taking the extra time with them. They shouldn't be neglected because of my personal issues."

"It's not a problem, Mrs. Montana. The boys are no trouble at all."

"I also want to say, though I appreciate your, um, services last night, I think it's best if we keep it on a purely professional level. I'd hate for things to become awkward or confusing. Plus the boys really love you, so I'd like to keep you as their nanny and only as their nanny. Do you understand?" Mercedes was a sweet girl, but there was no way anything like that could ever happen again. I already had one scandal going on; I didn't need a second.

"Yes, I understand, Mrs. Montana. I was just trying to help you relive so stress that's all."

"I appreciate you. I truly do. I'll be home shortly. Thank you." I ended the call and exhaled. I needed to think about how I wanted to present this information to Reggie. Before I was so angry, I 'd planned to hit him with everything I had, but now that I know that he isn't even aware of Nathaniel, how could I be mad? I'd had sex with Brooklyn on multiple occasions so how could I really be upset that he'd snuck off with LaNoir? She was throwing the ass at everybody back in the day and though I hated to admit it, Miriam was right; men would be men. They all seemed to have a wondering eye under the right circumstances. *A hard dick has no conscience and a wet pussy has few regrets,* my mother's voice rang in my head. My goal now was to see how we could keep our family together... including Nathaniel, without any drama from LaNoir and/or Brooklyn.

CHAPTER 14

*T*he next few days were grueling. I took part of Miriam's advice about not troubling Reggie with the revelation of his infidelity resulting in the production a child. A child that was now physically ill and needed his biological father. He had a multi-million-dollar case on the table and even though it was eating me alive, I couldn't mess that up. The ugly truth would just have to wait until he returned. I tried my best to keep things in order; giving my attention to my clients and the twins. I avoided unnecessary interactions with Mercedes and sent her home as soon as I arrived every evening. There wouldn't be any more sleepovers or extracurriculars. I was serious about maintaining a strictly professional relationship. I felt horrible smiling in the first lady's face when she stopped by the office Tuesday morning; she needed a personal assistant to help plan a surprise anniversary party for the pastor. I was probably on my way to hell in a hand-basket, but I didn't want it to be for allowing their daughter to suck my pussy dry.

Can we talk? A text from Brooklyn popped up on my phone.

I haven't had a chance to talk with Reggie. He'll be back in town tomorrow. I responded.

Brooklyn: Ok, but we still need to address a few things before he arrives.

Like what?

Brooklyn: Like you and LaNoir.

Fuck! I thought. He was right. I had no idea what Reggie knew about Brooklyn and I, if anything. If she could lie to her husband about Reggie knowing about his son, I wonder what she'd told him about me. *Yes, I think it's best if we all sat and talked before Reggie arrived so that we can be on the same page,* I responded. I figured Brooklyn needed to know that Reggie hadn't been avoiding them on purpose, but that it was in fact his wife's and Miriam's meddling who'd kept Reggie out of the loop.

Brooklyn: Cool, where do you want to do this at?

I thought about a restaurant, but if LaNoir was anything like she used to be I'm sure she had no qualms about causing a scene in public. My office wasn't an option; I had a few of my employees still assisting clients and I refuse to let anyone mess with my paper. I worked too hard to build a name for myself aside from the Montana's to have someone like LaNoir tear it down.

We can have complete privacy at my home, I texted him and included my address and he agreed to meet me there in an hour. That would give me enough time to get the boys squared away and have the staff prepare for guests. I didn't know how this was about to unfold, but I knew I couldn't avoid it any longer. LaNoir and I both had some explaining to do.

"Hey, Daddy is everything okay?" I knew it had to be something dealing with Gabriel for my father to be calling. The tropical storm happening on the coast sent us a ton of rain overnight and he was old school and didn't believe in making phone calls during a storm. Shit, he wouldn't even let us cut the television on as children. He would sit in the dark looking out of the window saying, "When God is doing His work, you be still." Gabriel and I would get our asses torn up if we didn't simmer down or even blinked too loud during a thunderstorm. "You should be praying and not playing," he'd say with a switch in his hand. He didn't like to be the disciplinarian, but mother wasn't the type to lay down rules and stick to them.

"Have you heard from Gabriel? He didn't come home last night." I could hear the concern in his voice.

"No, I haven't talked to Gabe since I came over on Sunday."

"If he got locked up he would've called by now."

"Well maybe he's laid up with Sarah Lee."

"Sandra Dee and naw she ain't seen or heard from him either. I asked when she came by and dropped off my food."

"Daddy I don't like that girl coming by like that. I can have a chef come and prepare you some fresh food… some healthy, fresh food every day."

"Why? That's just a waste of money. Ain't nothing wrong with that girl coming over here cookin'."

"Daddy, Gabe said she was one of Bishop's girls"--

"And."

"And Bishop is a pimp! Just because he has some of the prettiest girls working for him in those fake businesses doesn't mean he isn't a pimp, Daddy."

"That girl is with him 'cause she wanna be. Now I'm not saying it's right for her to be sellin' her coot like that but shit she ain't hurting for nothing. He keeps her dressed right. She got her own car and everything. She ain't on no street corner and she can cook her butt off. What she doin' ain't no secret. Some people slutin' out here living double lives and that ain't right either!" he yelled into the phone.

"Okay Daddy, okay. If I hear anything from Gabe, I'll be sure to let you know." I wasn't going to entertain that conversation any further. I already knew where it was headed, and I didn't want to upset him any more than what he was. I pulled into my driveway and saw Miriam's car parked in my spot and I rolled my eyes in disgust. She clearly didn't understand boundaries or just didn't give a fuck. *I swear to God if she had that decorator in my home again all hell was about to break loose,* I thought as I headed inside.

"Grace!" I called out when I saw no one present in the living room.

"Yes Mrs. Montana?" Grace called from the kitchen.

"Where is Miriam? I see her car outside," I questioned.

"She's with the twins, ma'am. She sent Mercedes home." I could tell by the tone in her voice that it was more to be said, but she fell silent when Miriam appeared down the stairs.

"Thank you, Grace. That will be all." Grace began to leave the room when I remembered Brooklyn and LaNoir would be arriving shortly. "Grace, please prepare the lounge. I have guests coming." She nodded her head and disappeared around the corner.

"Miriam I was hoping not to see you for a while," I sassed.

"And I was hoping my son would marry in his same class. It seems we are both cloaked in disappointment."

"Miriam what do you want? I know you didn't come over here just to see Chandler and Josiah so what is the issue now?"

"I came to make sure my son's home was presentable for his return. You haven't been in the best state of mind these last few days. I expect you to be fully attentive to his needs so that he doesn't suspect anything is awry."

"You know you have some nerve! Let's get things straight. This is my home. It may have been purchased with your money, but it's my name that's on the deed, so I don't want or need your help in telling me how MY home should be for MY husband. Second, I'm not keeping anything from him. It would hurt him more if he found out from someone else, God forbid, but what if something happened to that poor child and Reggie never got to meet him? That would kill him inside," I snapped.

"Are you done with your little rant?" Miriam pointed her submerged water looking finger at me. "Let me correct you. I don't have nerves I have balls, big ones! I am the one that keeps this family afloat and our dirty laundry buried as it should be. Without me the Montana legacy as you know it would have been chopped up and burnt on the grill years ago. When I see a problem, I pluck it out like a weed and you or no one else for that manner will be the cheap glue that falls apart and causes us to crumble. We accepted you into this family even though you're the spawn of a harlot. I gave you this beautiful home and I placed you in a circle of peers that you would never have been able to gain on your own. We gave you value and purpose and this is the thanks you give in return? You are going to cause a tidal wave of destruction so vicious that you will not be able to recover from if you don't do as I say and keep your mouth shut!" By the time she'd finished her cruel remarks she had her antique finger directly in my face. If I'd blinked I'm sure I would have felt it with my eyelash.

"Miriam get your ass out of my face!" I took a step back, glaring at her. "I don't care about what value you think you may have given me. I know I'm not perfect and I have made some horrible mistakes, but Reggie is a good man. I can forgive him for this child, but I will not be keeping this or any other secrets from him from now on!"

"Oh, that's right because you do have secrets, don't you?" Cruella Deville smirked. "So that means you plan on telling Reggie about your little affair?" She smiled so wide and so hard I thought her teeth would shatter from the pressure.

So, this 'A Wrinkle in Time' looking bitch did know about Brooklyn, I thought. "I'm sure Reggie and I can work through whatever, but we for damn sure will be doing it together and without your input." I had an abundance of choice words for the old cat in the hat, but the sound of the door-bell interjected my flow. *Shit! That must be Brooklyn and LaNoir.* I was so wrapped up in with the Grinch that I didn't realize what time it was. "Miriam you need to leave." I bolted towards the front cutting off Grace from opening the door. I swung the door so hard I was surprised it didn't come off the hinges. I was correct; there stood Brooklyn in this fitted hat pulled low over his eyes and LaNoir still dressed in a too small dress that screamed 'look at my tits.' She was still beautiful though; there was no denying that. Her chocolate skin looked like it was kissed by the sun. She resembled the rapper Foxy Brown and she hadn't aged a bit.

"Please come in. Miriam was just leaving." I shot invisible daggers at Miriam's head and prayed to God they punctured her throat, her eyes, her left nostril or something. Anything that would keep her from adding more unnecessary drama to the situation. As they stepped inside Miriam's face went from grim to gruesome. Her disgust was obvious and unapologetic.

"How dare you bring this trollop into my son's home!" she yelled

"Miriam get out!" I screamed.

She stormed over to LaNoir and grabbed her roughly by the arm. "You dirty little bitch! I told you to stay away from us!" she spazzed.

"If you don't get your hands off of me the hearse will be here to carry you off before your time. Which ain't that long." LaNoir rolled her neck so hard I swore I heard it crack.

"We had an agreement! You signed the papers! I'll sue you for everything you've got!" Miriam was outraged.

"That agreement won't stand in court! I took it to my own lawyer and he said that due to the circumstances I have a right to get the necessary information needed to save my son's life." Lanoir's words didn't help the situation. Miriam looked like a demon had possessed her body as she lunged at LaNoir. She grabbed her by her long black tresses and I hoped she didn't rip any of her scalp out but by the way LaNoir's head began to rock back and forth. I was sure she was going to be bald in several spots. They fell out the door and rolled out onto the porch and down the stairs with Miriam taking most of the steps into her back. She might have been an old bitch, but that grey goose was wearing LaNoir's ass out!

Brooklyn sprang into action trying to pry Thing one and Thing two apart. Miriam unleased her blows on him as well. *Bip, bip, bip, bip!* I guess she thought, fuck it, anyone could get it. I wondered if she had private training classes with Ali back in the day because she was giving him the business. This had to be the wildest shit I had ever been through. Never in a million years would I have thought, I'd be a witness to Miriam Montana, aka Ms. Perfect, rolling around in her expensive suit with anyone, let alone LaNoir, giving Brooklyn a KFC style combo. I didn't even try to stop this shit show. I just took a seat on the stairs as the staff piled up outside like a heard of farm animals at feeding time. Brooklyn held LaNoir back with one hand while trying to block the blows Miriam was dishing.

"WHAT THE FUCK IS GOING ON!" Reggie screamed as he ran up, grabbing his mother. Everything unfolded so fast I hadn't noticed he'd pulled up in the driveway.

CHAPTER 15

"GET THE FUCK OFF OF MY MOTHER! Brooklyn what the fuck are you and LaNoir doing here? What the fuck is going on!" Reggie demanded answers while stepping in front of Miriam trying the shield her. I was in total shock as I stood but couldn't form any words to explain why his mother was giving out two pieces like it was lunchtime. She really was tagging the fuck out of Brooklyn's head.

"CALL THE POLICE! CALL THE POLICE! I want these hoodlums arrested for assault!" Miriam yelled over Reggie's shoulder, shaking her withered fist.

"Bitch you attacked me!" LaNoir belted as she tried placing her hanging track hair back on her head. It was several pieces laying in the front yard as well.

"Oh, that shit gone," one of the staffers whispered.

"Um-hm she gonna have to call her stylist for that," another added.

"Everyone needs to leave!" I instructed when I realized all of them were beginning to whisper. This is the second time in less than a week I had ordered everyone off my property. A few of them hesitated and began to mumble under their breath like I couldn't hear them talking about me. "If you want to have a mother fucking job tomorrow I suggest you get your shit and go home!" I spat.

"Oh, you ain't got to tell me twice."

"Welp time to go."

"I wanted to leave early anyway," I heard some of them say.

Even though this wasn't the way I wanted to reveal my findings to Reggie, it was what it was and there was nothing I could do about it. There would be no sugar coating, only raw, hard facts, because everyone wanted answers.

"I still need to know why the fuck Brooklyn and LaNoir is here and fighting my mother!" Reggie was confused and breathing heavily. Hell, they all were. Miriam looked like a cat soaked in water. LaNoir was damn near bald on one side of her head and Brooklyn should have changed his name to Willy Lump-lump. It was obvious we needed to wait until all the help had depleted and that's exactly what we did. Miriam and Reggie walked inside first. I motioned for Brooklyn to go in next with LaNoir following.

"Mommy what's going on?" Chandler's tiny frightened voice crept down the stairs.

"Mommy I'm scared," Josiah cried out.

"Everything's okay boys, I promise," I called back. "Please go in your rooms and I'll be up in a second."

"But I'm scared! Can we watch a movie in your room?" Josiah begged as he began taking steps down the stairs.

"Yes! But only if you go right now."

The boys scurried off down the hall. I didn't say a word until I heard their footsteps go quiet. "Reggie what are you doing here? We weren't expecting you until tomorrow." I walked towards him.

"I was trying to surprise you, but clearly I'm the one who got hit with the surprise. Can someone please tell me what the fuck is going on?" Confusion was written all over his face.

"Look man this is not what we came here for. We've been trying to get in touch with you about Nathaniel and everything just went south," Brooklyn said.

"Nathaniel? Who the fuck is Nathaniel? Reggie polled.

"Fuck you mean? Who is Nathaniel?" Brooklyn's face now mirrored Reggie's. "Look I already told Sadie everything, so you don't have to front for her. We just want what's best for our son." Brooklyn pulled LaNoir close to him.

"Your son? Brooklyn, I haven't seen or heard from you in years. How am I supposed to know you have a son and what does he have to do with you squabbling in my damn front yard with my mother?"

"Yo, are you playing games with me right now?" Brooklyn stood and took a step towards Reggie. "This isn't a fuckin' joke! I just told you Sadie knows everything, so you can stop with the fake amnesia, bruh." Brooklyn's voice became aggressive.

"And I just told you I had no idea you have a son, let alone what his name is partna!" Reggie took a step towards Brooklyn and it was obvious these two were about to exchange blows themselves if LaNoir or Miriam didn't step in and reveal the ugly truth.

"Miriam? LaNoir? This would be your cue," I interjected.

"Reggie, baby, it's nothing you need to worry yourself with. Let your mother take care of this, please darling," Miriam begged.

"Look there's something I need to tell you." LaNoir kept her eyes on the ground as she spoke.

"There's nothing you need to tell him!" Miriam shouted and lunged at LaNoir again, but Reggie grabbed her by the arm keeping her in place.

"Tell me what?" Reggie looked at her then at me trying to piece things together in his head.

"Yeah tell him what?" Brooklyn took his arm of protection from around LaNoir's back. "You told me he knew everything and the only person who didn't know was Sadie, but I took care of that so that there would be no more secrets between everyone."

"Tell him, LaNoir," I encouraged.

"It's not him who I have something to tell," she whispered. Tears began to flow from her eyes and down her cheeks, but she still didn't lift her head. "I'm sorry, Brooklyn."

"Sorry for what?" Brooklyn questioned. "Sorry for what LaNoir?" Brooklyn's voice began to crack as emotion filled his throat.

"Reggie isn't Nathaniel's father," she revealed. The room went dead silent for a few seconds. We all were dazed and confused except for Miriam. She looked like she had to shit a load of bricks.

"What the fuck!" Reggie let Miriam go.

"What the fuck did you just say?" Brooklyn spoke softly. His demeanor had changed from angry to calm in the worst way.

"Yeah, what the fuck did you just say?" I repeated, crossing my arms like a mad school teacher.

"I'm sorry! I'm so sorry it had to come to this, but I had no choice!" LaNoir finally looked up into Brooklyn's eyes.

"Wait, can someone clarify what the fuck she's talking about? Why the fuck would you tell him I had a baby by you? I've never had sex with you! I would NEVER have sex with you!" Reggie fumed.

"I know and I'm sorry! I'm sooo sorry Reggie, but I had no choice! Miriam was determined to keep me quiet and she gave us all that money! I wouldn't even be here if Nathaniel didn't get sick. I told her about his illness and she didn't care! She didn't care if my baby lived or died and this was the only way I could get him the help he needs! Brooklyn, baby, I'm sorry! Baby I'm so sorry baby, but you have to understand I did this for us!" LaNoir blubbered.

"For us? How did you do this for us? You've been taking these people's money and Nathaniel isn't even Reggie's son! What the fuck is wrong with you? Who is the father? Huh LaNoir! WHO THE FUCK IS MY SON'S FATHER!" Brooklyn was falling apart. His anger had returned and blossomed into full-blown rage. I saw fear enter LaNoir's eyes as she shot a glance over to Miriam. We all followed suit and stared at Miriam waiting for her to open her mouth. She stared off into space as if she was oblivious to us being in the room with her.

"My husband," she finally spoke after what seemed like forever.

"What the hell?" I blurted.

"Mother, what did you just say?" Reggie questioned while rubbing his hands over his head repeatedly.

"You heard me. My husband, your father, ran his dick up in that whore and got her pregnant!" She snatched her purse off the coffee table and stormed off towards the front door. "This is all your fault!"

she snarled, pointing her beef jerky like finger into my face. "Ever since you came into our lives I've been having to clean up the messes you've made!"

"Fuck this shit!" Brooklyn pulled his keys out of his pocket and bolted out the front door. LaNoir ran after him pleading and begging for his forgiveness, but that didn't dull his steps.

"Mother get your hand out of her face!" Reggie stood in between us. "Sadie had nothing to do with this bullshit you and LaNoir put together," he defended.

"Sadie has everything to do with this! I told you not to marry this Jezebel, but you just had to have her! If you would have left her when I told you she spread her legs for your best friend we wouldn't be here right now!" she snapped. Shock waves filled my body. I didn't know Reggie was aware of my dealings with Brooklyn. It was clear this family tried to bury anything that was unsightly.

"Just leave!" Reggie demanded.

"Just leave? How dare you try to kick me out of the house I paid for! She's the one who needs to leave!"

"Mother this is my wife!"

"Your wife? Ha! What kind of wife is she? I'll tell you what kind! She's the kind that lets your best friend stuff her full of raw meat minutes before she walks down the aisle! She's the type that hangs around with skanks that throws themselves at your father at your engagement party! She's the type that lets the children's sitter fondle her while she's too damn drunk to be a mother to them!"

"What? What the fuck is she talkin' about?" Reggie glanced back at me.

"Look, we need to talk," was all I could muster. *How in the hell did she know about Mercedes?*

"You see! She doesn't even deny it! You think I don't know everything that goes on in this family! I had this house built for y'all from the ground up, but I knew this hussy couldn't be trusted so I had cameras installed in every room! I couldn't believe my eyes when I played the feedback today and saw that wicked girl placing her mouth between your thighs. And to think she's the pastor's daughter!" Miriam confessed.

"Wait what? You did what? You have cameras in our home and you didn't think to discuss this with me!" Reggie was outraged, and rightfully so. Miriam was the Houdini of deception. This nursing -home-ready bitch had more tricks than the cereal. When she realized she'd slip up, she tried to backpedal and downplay the situation.

"Reggie, I did what I had to do to make sure you were being properly taken care of."

"Mother you need to go!"

"Reggie darling, please just let me explain. I'm the reason this family stays together as a unit and out of the newspapers!"

"You are the reason for a lot of things mother. Sadie is my wife. My wife! And I'll be damned if you or anyone else put her down in my presence. I'm not perfect and you know about most of my troubles, so I dare you to try to belittle the woman I love. Get out of OUR home!" Reggie spoke with conviction and Miriam knew he meant every single word. She didn't bat an eye before walking out and slamming the front door behind her.

Reggie turned to me and said, "I guess it's time we talk." And I couldn't have agreed more.

CHAPTER 16

*R*eggie and I sat through three and a half hours of questions and answers after he got the boys ready for bed. He wanted to spend some time with them and be in calm state of mind before we had a much-needed heart-to-heart. I told him everything that happened in the coat-room and how Brooklyn was fed the story that he had sex with LaNoir in retaliation for it. I told him how Miriam lead me to believe that she hadn't told him about my sexual sexcapade with Brooklyn to try to use as leverage in an attempt to keep my mouth closed. Sorrow and regret almost suffocated my mind when I confessed the horrible secrets I'd been harboring. I even explained the situation with Mercedes while he was away. He took the information much better than I'd expected seeing that he also had secrets of his own that needed to be revealed. He confessed that he'd cheated on me with two different women. One before we got married and one during, after his mother revealed what the wedding coordinator had witnessed; that bitch.

"Mercedes can no longer work here," Reggie said, and I had no choice but to agree. "That some shit waiting to happen. Not that it can't get much worse at this point."

"I'll take her out for lunch tomorrow and let her know."

Reggie nodded his head. "I need to take a shower," he spoke softly then went into the restroom. I heard the shower turn on and I contemplated getting in with him. I knew he was hurting not just because of me, but Miriam really showed out tonight. He loved his parents so seeing their picture-perfect image tarnished was heartbreaking for him. I followed my gut and disrobed. I walked into out oversized restroom and peered at my husband through the glass shower door. His back was turned towards me with his head lowered. I hadn't seen Reggie shed a tear since the twins were born, but I could tell by the way his shoulders jerked that my lover was in pain. I startled him as I stepped inside the walk-in shower, hugging him from behind. He cuffed his hands around mine and accepted the embrace.

"I'm so sorry Reggie," I apologized again, and I meant every word. Lust was what I had with Brooklyn, but that could never compare to the love that had developed between Reggie and I. I hated that I didn't realize it sooner, but I knew that if we could sit there listening to every single unpleasant detail that the other shared and we still saw love when we looked into each other's eyes, we would be able to make it through any storm.

He turned around slowly and sat down on the built-in seat. "I know Sadie baby, I know." He grabbed my hands and I dropped to my knees instantly. My tears fell simultaneously with his as the warm water from the shower head sprinkled on my bare chest. Here we were naked, but not just in the physical sense. We'd exposed our souls, shedding light on the ugly truth. Hidden secrets buried at the end of a dark tunnel finally revealed. I looked into my husband's eyes and I saw the pain I'd caused, and it killed me inside. I wondered in that moment if my mother hadn't died that day and was somehow able to run back to my father would she have told him the ugly truth. Would she have exposed her secret lust for a man that didn't want her beyond the curves of her body and see that my father, her husband, would love her unconditionally?

I searched his eyes for reassurance and the delicate touch of his hand on my cheek comforted my spirit. He leaned forward kissing me deeply. I'd never felt anything close to that single kiss at that moment from Reggie. He literally took my breath away as he pulled me in to his embrace. He wrapped his arms around me and I became lost in his touch. I felt his manhood growing as it poked at the top of stomach in between my breasts. Cuffing my them together I squeezed my juicy mounds around his stiff dick and began to slowly stroke his shaft. His dick head poked me in the chin before taking all of it into my mouth. He needed this release. Hell, he deserved it. I swirled my tongue around his swollen top and a heard a sigh escape his lips. I stared in his eyes as I slid up and down on his shaft. The water beat down on my back as he leaned against the wall, relaxing as he watched me perform.

I slurped on his pole and began to moan. I was actually enjoying pleasuring my man as much as he enjoyed receiving it. Reggie stretched his legs and I could feel his thigh muscles beginning to flex. I worked my jaws effortlessly. Up, down, up, down, only pulling his meat out to slap it on my lips as I stroked his shaft with my hand. I hadn't sucked his dick with this much effort in months. I felt him jerk and then his eyes rolled in the back of his head. He blew his load into my mouth and I swallowed every drop. I stood, preparing to exit the shower when he pulled me towards him.

He grabbed his long throbbing dick and whispered, "We're not finished yet." Grabbing my right thigh, he guided me to sit on his lap. I was surprised to see he was still brick hard because he usually needed time to recover if there was a round two. I rested my hands on his shoulders as he pierced Yoni and she began quivering as her walls adjusted to his wood. "Sadie baby,"—he whispered in my ear as his hands cuffed my ass cheeks, spreading them apart. – "tell me you love me."

"I love you Reggie."

"Tell me you need me."

"I need you baby, I need you."

"Now tell me you want me." His voice cracked, and I could feel the pain as he spoke.

"I want you Reggie. I want our family, and I want us."

"I love you Lady Sadie, I love you," he repeated those words over and over until I began to shake. My pussy creamed as I began to cum all over his dick. He grunted and bit my neck before shooting his warm cum into my gushing hole. I sat there on top of my husband dripping wet from our love as well as the water that flowed down our bodies. We soaped each other down slowly caressing each other as the suds formed. After we'd dried off we climbed into bed and he held me close to his heart all night.

Morning came swiftly, and I'd already called my employee's prior to inform them I wasn't coming in since I was expecting Reggie to return today instead of last night. I wondered how things went with Brooklyn and LaNoir once they left, but I refused to call to find out. They needed time to work out their own shit.

"I think I'm going to see my father today," Reggie said as he fastened the last button on his Thom Browne dress shirt. He looked so handsome even though there was still sorrow lingering his eyes, but this pain wasn't caused by me. No, this was the pain of a broken child who just realized his superheroes didn't actually have mystical powers. They were just regular people who made human mistakes but put on a good show.

"Do you want me to come with you? I can ask Grace to keep an eye on the boys and after I meet with Mercedes, we can link up and go to your parent's house together," I proposed.

Reggie thought for a second then agreed. "I have a few things to do at the office. Just call me when you're through." He kissed me sweetly on the lips then headed downstairs. I heard the boys greeting him before he headed out.

"Grace, I need you to look after Josiah and Chandler while I run a few errands. I will also need you to watch them the rest of the week until I can find a replacement since Mercedes will no longer be working here. I'll compensate you for your trouble."

"It's no trouble. I don't mind taking care of these two. They remind me of my grandsons." Grace smiled as she placed their breakfast on the table. "You go, get out of here. They will be fine." She smiled again.

"Thank you, Grace. I really appreciate your help and discretion. These last few days have been trying."

"Oh, I know. You just go, and we will be fine."

I kissed the twins on their foreheads, grabbed my bag and headed out the door, but was startled to see Gabriel standing there.

CHAPTER 17

"Gabe what's wrong?" I asked as I pulled the door closed behind me. It was unlike him to show up at my home let alone without calling prior.

"Why does something have to be wrong?" His demeanor clearly showed something wasn't right. The way he kept looking over his shoulder made me weary.

"Because you never come to my home. The only time I see you is at Dad's. By the way have you talked to him? He's worried about you."

"Nah, I haven't had the chance to call. Sandra goes by almost every day to makes sure he eats and has the shit he needs when I'm making runs tho."

"Yeah we need to talk about that. I don't like her over there around Daddy. It seems like you could be around more if you stayed out of the streets. When are you going to stop all this foolishness and get yourself together Gabe?"

"Get myself together? Who the fuck do you think you're talking to? The last time I checked it was my money that helped send your uppity ass to school so that you could meet this rich mutha fuckah and live this baller life. We weren't dealt the same cards little sis. I make sure Pops eats, gets his meds and keeps his doctor's appoint-

96

ments when he talks about giving up. You pop in here and there, but let's not act like you're the one washing his dirty draws," he snapped.

"Look, I'm not trying to piss you off. All I'm saying is that you could be so much better than what you are. I offered to move Daddy in my house, but he refused. I even told him I could get him a personal chef and y'all could use our car service, but you know how he is. He doesn't want to feel like he's a bother. I even offered to send you to school for mechanic work or anything you wanted to do, but you'd rather be making runs for Bishop." I rolled my eyes.

"As long as Pops is taken care of, don't worry about what the fuck I be doing."

"Easier said than done when Daddy has to call me every other month to bail your ass out of jail."

"HE called you and asked you to do that. I've never called you once and asked you for shit. The one thing I asked you for you acted all shady like usual, but that's you though. Ol' shady Sadie."

"What did you ask me for Gabe?"

"I asked you for ol' girl's number. The chocolate shorty that watches the boys for you."

"Mercedes? Oh, hell no! That girl is sweet and doesn't need to be corrupted by you."

"See that's that shit I'm talking about! Perfect example of how you think you're better than me. How do you want me to do better but you won't introduce me to better people?"

"You can't be serious. I don't think I'm better than anyone. I went to school and earned my degree. I passed those classes and yes, I married into a family with money, but even if I hadn't I always had a business plan. Introducing you to new people won't mean shit if you are still associating with old ways."

"I'm trying Sadie, damn. I know I fucked up when I got involved with Bishop, but you know how he his. I can't just up and quit until I pay my dues." He shifted his weight from one leg to the other and looked over his shoulder again.

"Gabriel you still haven't told me why you are here. Is everything okay?"

"Yeah, I'm cool. I honestly just came over to see if you had any leads on some legit jobs. Hard to go straight when you have a record."

I searched his face to see if he there was an ounce of sincerity. This was out of the ordinary for him, just showing up and asking me for help was slightly bafflingly. I'd tried on many occasions to help Gabriel get his life on track, but he always acted like he resented me. *If Reggie could forgive then so could I. Everyone deserves a second chance,* I thought. "I can put in a good word with a few associates I know that work with offenders, but you can't fuck this up Gabe. My name means everything to me."

"I know, I know, and I won't. I promise." He gave a half-ass smile, but I figured it was hard for him to ask me for help seeing that I was his little sister. If he wanted a better life, I would do everything in my power to make sure he had a fair shot.

Beep! Beep! I looked down at my phone and saw I had a text from Mercedes: *Are we still on?*

"Shit! Look I have to go. I'm running late for an appointment," I told Gabriel as I walked past him and got into my car.

"Are the boys inside with their nanny? I wanted to see them before I left."

"They are with Grace. I have to find another sitter," I said as I rolled the car windows down. I preferred fresh air over the ac.

"Damn, what happened to ol' girl?"

"She just isn't going to work out. I'm on my way to her now to tell her I have to let her go."

"Well shit let me ride with you then." He walked over and hopped onto the passenger seat.

"Gabe this is a business meeting not love connection. That girl is only nineteen years old anyway what could you possibly want with her?"

"You act like I'm an old-ass pervert or something. Nineteen sounds like the right age to me. She's legal, fine as hell, and she must be smart if you hired her. She doesn't have all these preconceived notions about men and shit, plus I'm hungry."

"What does your hunger have to do with me?"

"I know you. All ya business meetings involve food or drinks. I'm hoping for both." He grinned.

"Then eat a snickers."

"Damn Sadie c'mon! I thought you wanted to see me win?" He grinned harder and I caved. After all he hardly ever came to my home, so he must have been serious about trying to become a better version of himself.

"Look you can ride, but I'm serious about Mercedes. Leave that girl alone." I buckled my seat belt and texted Mercedes that I was on my way.

"Yo what the fuck is this shit?" Gabe pointed to the radio.

"*Uh,* music." I'd expanded my musical tastes from hood classics and trap music to lighter interests.

"This is some old Banana Republic type shit," he insulted.

"Good music is good music." I shrugged.

"But this ain't good music." He laughed

"What? I like Iggy."

"Oh my God is that who this is?" Gabe acted like he melted in his seat, covering his face with his hands. "That bitch is the worst, hands down."

"So, who do you propose I listen to then?"

Gabriel retrieved his phone from his pocket and with a few taps to the screen we were vibin' to the beat.

"Okay, okay. I can rock with it. Who is that?"

"Shit that's the homie Kassius Brikkz. He did that joint, 'Kurvz' with all the BBW chicks clappin' their asses in the video. Shiiiidd I'm tryna get to one of those Bunnies and Dons parties he be hostin' and shit." It was cool being able to just chill with my brother. I can't remember a time since our mother passing that he even wanted to be around me longer than a few minutes. It was refreshing to know that we could finally share the same place without taking shots at each other. This was the big brother I missed.

I pulled into Catalina's and reminded Gabe that this wasn't a dating game. I seriously needed to handle things with Mercedes without a hiccup. She was sitting at a table by a window and already ordered her food. I asked Gabe to wait at the bar, so I could talk with her privately.

"Please excuse my tardiness," I said as I took a seat across from the dark brown bombshell. She really was naturally gorgeous.

"Oh, it's okay. I was starving so I went ahead an ordered," she said pointing at her plate. "Would you like for me to call the waitress back to take your order as well?

"No, I won't be here that long. Look I need to be frank. I thought that I could go on pretending like this weekend didn't happen, but I can't. I think it's best if we part business altogether."

She stopped eating and a look of disappointment took over her face. "Oh, I see. Mrs. Montana, I want to apologize. I took advantage of a situation and I knew I'd cross the line, but I thought that you might have liked the time that we shared."

"Mercedes I am a married woman. Regardless of whether I enjoyed it or not that's not something I wished to have happened. Chandler and Josiah are going to have a fit when I tell them you will no longer be their sitter. It hurts me that my babies are going to be hurt, but Reggie said"—

"Reggie? You mean Mr. Montana knows?" Her eyes widened as she gasped and began to cough. She was choking on the grilled chicken she'd held in her mouth.

"Oh my gosh! Are you okay?" I offered her some water, but she gave me the signal that she was choking. I jumped up and started patting her on the back.

"Help! Help! Can someone help me please! She's choking!" I yelled. I was freaking out. I wanted to let her go peacefully, not have her die at the table. Gabriel sat his glass down at the bar and rushed over to assist. He grabbed Mercedes like a rag doll and began doing the Heimlich maneuver. Four strong hunches later the chicken popped out of her mouth and landed on my silver red bottoms.

"Is she okay? Should I call the ambulance?" the clearly shaken waitress asked as she gripped the phone tightly in her hand.

"I'm fine. I just need some water," Mercedes managed to say in a strained voice.

I grabbed the glass of lemon water off the table and pushed it into her hands. She took a few sips then exhaled slowly. She slowly began to look like her normal self again.

"Oh my God! You scared me!" I confessed.

"I'm okay, really I am. Thank you, sir," Mercedes reached out to shake Gabriel's hand.

"Oh, no problem baby girl. I told my sister I wanted to meet you, but I didn't know I'd be saving your life on our first date."

"Wait what?" Mercedes started coughing again.

"Dammit Gabriel, leave this girl alone! You're gonna make her choke again." I rubbed her back and pushed her to drink some more water.

"My bad little momma. I was making a joke. Are you okay?" Gabe pulled out her chair and encouraged her to take a seat.

"Mercedes you remember my brother Gabriel, don't you?" I asked as I took my seat. Gabe sat in a chair beside her.

"I thought he looked familiar, but it was hard to place his face while trying to breathe." She laughed.

"I was just telling my sister on the ride over that I'd like to take you out sometime. Hopefully, we can get familiar."

I wrinkled my nose in disgust. I specifically told that negro not to push up on her and here he was trying to turn the charm on after she almost met Jesus from a piece of poultry.

"Hey love, I got a little caught up at the restaurant, but I'm on my way," I told Reggie after answering his call. He needed me, and I'd spent more time than I planned with Mercedes. "I promise I'm on my way. See you soon." I hung up the phone and debated if I had enough time to drop Gabe off at home. I reached in my bag and laid a card on the table. This was going to be another hard day for my husband and I needed to be by his side. "Look, I have to meet Reggie so here's the number to the car service. Have them drop you off at my house so you can get your truck. Mercedes are you sure you're okay?" I was truly concerned, but I needed to go be with my husband.

"Yes, I'm good."

"I hate that I had to let you go, but I'll provide you any references you need," I assured her as I placed a hundred-dollar bill on the table. That would cover her lunch and proved a nice tip for the waitress.

"It's okay Mrs. Montana. And you don't have to do that. I can pay." She tried to hand me back the bill but was intercepted by Gabriel.

"First rule of the game; always take the money." He smiled and placed the bill back on the table. I shot his ass a wicked glare and wished I had time to drop his thirsty ass at home. I grabbed my purse and speed walked out the door.

"I'm on my way baby. I'm on my way."

CHAPTER 18

We walked hand in hand into the Montana estate, passing the perfectly contoured hedges. I took notice to the saint statues that lined the driveway leading up to the bubbling fountain. *They must have added those recently,* I thought as I squeezed Reggie's hand tightly. Miriam and Reggie Sr. really had elaborate taste, though I'm sure ninety percent of the décor was upon Miriam's demand. Image was everything to Miriam Elizabeth Montana and on a scale of one to ten, their estate screamed millions.

"Good afternoon, Sir," Jonas the butler greeted.

"Good afternoon, Jonas." Reggie nodded in acknowledgment.

"You are looking rather delightful Mrs. Montana if I do say," Jonas complemented.

"It's Sadie, Jonas you know that. How is Ava doing? I apologize for not stopping by the hospital, but I hope you received the flowers I sent."

"She is doing quite well, thank you for asking and yes she beamed when she saw the beautiful bouquet you sent over. Lilies are her favorite." He smiled as he took my hand helping me step down into the foyer. "I shall go inform your parents of your arrival," Jonas announced, then disappeared down the long hallway.

"I see mother has done some redecorating," Reggie mumbled as he ran his fingers across the base of the Harcourt Baluster vase that adorned the mantle above the fireplace.

"May I offer you a beverage, ma'am?" Willena the maid offered.

"No thank you, Willena, but can you bring Reggie a glass of chilled water please." I placed my purse on the Jay Strongwater floral side table, accidentally knocking over a decorative bottle.

"Oh my gosh you have to be careful!" Miriam snapped as she ran over forcefully retrieving the glasswork from my hand.

"I'm sorry Miriam it was an accident."

"Everything is an accident with you," she snarled.

"Mother, I came over here to talk with you and father, but I will leave if you think you're going to disrespect my wife. I thought we got this cleared up last night." Reggie stepped directly into Miriam path. As nasty as she was, Reggie had her heart. He was her miracle baby, so I knew damaging him was the last thing she wanted to do even though she did a damn good job of it last night.

"Reggie, I've been through the storm and I can't take her being here in my presence. I think it's best if she leaves."

"You can't possibly be serious. Where's father? I want to talk to him. I have questions that need answers," Reggie insisted.

"Your father doesn't want to see anyone at this moment. You'll just have to come back later... and alone." She dismissed his request and began walking back down the hall to the stairwell.

"Mother! I said I want to speak with my father and I want to see him now!" Reggie's voice boomed throughout the corridor.

Miriam looked as if a vein had busted in her neck. "You want to see you father? Fine go and see him, but I warn you, you will not find your precious father up those stairs." She was clearly tired of protecting Reggie, from what I don't know, but the level of disgust became undeniable as she walked over to the liquor cabinet and poured herself a drink and gulped it down.

"What is that supposed to mean? Where's father?" Reggie's voice morphed from angry to concerned.

"Oh, he's up there. Go see for yourself." She poured another drink and walked off into the kitchen.

I looked at Reggie as worry became present. "Would you like me to come with you?" I asked.

"No. Just wait here for me please." He went up the split staircase and disappeared down the right wing. Willena walked over and handed me the glass of water I'd requested for Reggie.

"Thank you."

"What are you thanking her for? That's my water you're holding, purchased with my money. You should be thanking me." Miriam walked back into the room with a different glass filled with what I assumed was another alcoholic beverage. She rolled her dark brown eyes as she bypassed Willena.

"It's called being polite." I wasn't in the mood for any more of Miriam's shit.

"And what would you know about that? It's apparent your father didn't teach you any manners. If he had, you'd be grateful for the life-style my son has provided you with instead of bringing drama into his life."

"Look just stop it okay. All of this has nothing to do with what you and LaNoir hatched out. I'm just here to support my husband." I took a sip of the water.

Miriam took a seat on her cream, high-back chair and laughed. "Support, ha! Do you know that the water you're drinking costs four hundred and two dollars per bottle? *Hm?* Kona Nigari, that's what it's called. It's harvested two thousand feet below the surface of the Pacific Ocean of Hawaii. I have to have it shipped here from Japan because they don't sell it anywhere else. Did you know that?"

"What does that have to do with anything?" I was becoming annoyed.

"I'm trying to give you a much-needed lesson about hierarchy. Somehow you've seemed to have the order of things out of place."

I didn't want to fuel another outburst, so I stood quietly and listened.

"Do you know why I go through great lengths to have the very best? Because I've earned it! I've put up with so much to keep this family afloat. You think scandals don't come with this lifestyle? Everyone wants a piece of what you have and they're willing to sacrifice your family to do it! What are you going to do when these little young tramps throw themselves at your husband? And I'm not talking about those workplace sluts that try to fuck the boss for a raise. I'm referring to the professional con artists that like to take photos and blackmail you for thousands of dollars to keep quiet about your man's unique fetishes."

I didn't know what to say. As much as I didn't want to admit it, I slightly felt sorry for Miriam.

"I gave my all to that man!" she cried. "I suffered and almost died trying to give him a son even though I wanted a daughter, but I never got the chance to even try for another baby. Just like that everything that made me a woman was pulled out! And do you think he cares about my pain? Do you think he even asked me how I was feeling after being told I'd never be able to get my precious baby girl? No! He was on the way to Indiana before I could close my eyes to sleep. Sorry bastard." Miriam's voice grew heavy. I didn't know if it was because of all the liquor that she'd consumed, or if she finally wanted to talk about their family secrets she'd hidden so well over the years. It was probably a combination of both, but either way I was all ears.

"I made a vow to always protect Reggie because if he knew the man his father really was it would destroy him. I did a damn good job of it too until your yella ass came along. Now he's up there with that shell of a man and when he returns down those steps I have bear witness to the heartbreak in my baby's eyes. I just want you to see what you did. What pain you brought into his life all because you couldn't keep your filthy mouth closed. Do you know that LaNoir isn't the only one?" Miriam took a big gulp from her glass and set it on the table so hard I thought it would have busted.

"What are you talking about?"

"LaNoir, that black bitch you called a friend. You know that's something I don't understand either." Her words began to slur. "How did you ever have a whore like that as a friend? *Hm?* Oh, I know!

Because you're a little sleazy whore too! You fucked your best friend's man which was also your husband's best friend and you couldn't have cared less. Isn't it amazing how we can conceal things when it benefits us, but want to point at the other person and call them wrong for doing the same? I just wanted to keep my family together and happy. I could have dealt with LaNoir and that lil' nappy-headed child of hers. Hell, I've been taking care of all of Reggie's siblings for years so what would be any different with this one?"

I was astonished by Miriam's revelations, but before I could part my lips to speak Reggie came rushing down the stairs.

"Reggie are you okay?" I asked.

"Well that's a stupid question. Look at him! Clearly he's not o-kay. What? Did Daddy's baby finally find out who his hero really is?" she taunted.

"Get your bag and let's go!" he demanded.

I grabbed my bag and we hurried out the front door. I could see tears falling from Reggie's eyes before we reached our cars.

"You shouldn't drive. Get in my car and we can send for yours later," I suggested.

"No, I'm fine!"

"No, you're not. Reggie please let me help you," I begged.

"I said I'm fine!" he snapped.

I stood there in silence not knowing what happened when he walked up those stairs; not knowing what was said that made him break down like this. I wanted to reach out and hold him in my arms, but instead I just stood there.

"Sadie, listen. I didn't' mean to snap at you, but I'm just ready to get away from this place. I can drive myself just follow me out and we can discuss everything at home."

Against my better judgment I agreed to his request and I got into my car. Before I could turn the key in the ignition my phone rang. "Hello Daddy."

"Sadie have you heard from Gabriel?"

"I saw Gabe earlier. He dropped by my house and I told him to call you."

"I haven't heard from him and I haven't seen that girl Sandra either."

"She didn't come by to make sure you got your lunch?"

"I haven't seen her since yesterday."

"What? Daddy when's the last time you ate?"

"Yesterday. But I had a can of wienies and crackers on my table, so I ate those for breakfast."

"See that's exactly why I said I didn't want that girl there. Anyone dealing with Gabriel isn't reliable." I was pissed.

"Calm down, calm down. I'm a little hungry, but I'm not dead. I am in a little bit of pain though. I can't take my medication until I eat, or it'll make me sick."

"Daddy I'm on my way," I reassured him then hung up the phone. I dialed Reggie to let him know I needed to go by my father's before I headed home. It rang several times then went to voicemail. I tried calling again but got the same result. "Shit," I mumbled. I decided to send him a text instead. I figured he had the music blasting to soothe his pain and couldn't hear the phone ringing.

Babe, I have to stop by my Dad's to fix him some lunch and to make sure he has his meds. Be home soon, luv you.

I tossed my phone on the passenger's seat and pulled out of the driveway. As I drove I replayed Miriam's words in my head. I wondered how many illegitimate children Reggie Sr. had floating around and why Miriam didn't leave his ass. Hell, who was I kidding? I knew exactly why she didn't leave him. But there was no way I'd let Reggie have two or more babies on me. It didn't take long for me to reach my father's and I had him comfortable and eating within minutes. I made a mental note to call my chef and have him prepare some meals that were healthy and easy to make just in case Gabriel pulled one of these fast ones again. That reminded me I needed to call him and chew his ass out for leaving Daddy stuck like this.

CHAPTER 19

"**W**HO THE FUCK IS THIS!" a strange voice barked in my ear. I had to look at my screen to ensure I'd called the right number.

"Who is this? Where's Gabe?"

"Man fuck that nigga Gabe!"

I stared at my phone in disbelief. Was this a joke? If it was it wasn't funny. "Look I don't know who you are, but I need to talk to my brother. Stop playing around and give him his phone."

"Bitch fuucckkk you! Fuck that nigga Gabe and fuck that lil' chocolate hoe he was with."

"Wait what? Mercedes? Is she with him? Put my brother on the phone right now!" I demanded.

"Look you waffle-headed hoe. What don't you understand? This is my phone now and you can ligg-ma."

"Ligg-ma? What is ligg-ma?"

"LICK MA BALLS BITCH!" The voice on the other end erupted in laughter then the phone went silent. He'd hung up in my face and when I tried calling back I got sent to voicemail. I tried calling Mercedes number, but I got no answer either.

"Daddy I have to go. I'll be back tonight to make sure you have dinner." I kissed him on the head then sprinted out the door. I tried calling Mercedes phone again but still got no answer. "Fuck! What the hell is going on?" I thought about calling her parents, but I didn't want to alarm them if she was just out partying or something. Running around with Gabe anything was possible. I shot her a text instructing her to call me as soon as she got my message. I knew it was a bad idea to allow Gabriel to come with me to that restaurant. Something in my stomach told me not to bring him, but I didn't listen. I was worried about Mercedes and kept dialing her phone all the way home. I became so obsessed with getting her to answer I almost lost control of my car when I hit a sharp curve. "Oh my God!" I screamed as I yanked the steering wheel to avoid running off the street into the woods. If I'd gone any faster, I would have slid into the multiple police officers that were just around the corner. Sadly, someone else had lost control and ran into a tree. The officers were directing cars to bypass the incident safely. As I crept around the EMS truck my heart began to pound profusely. It felt like I was about to have a heart attack when I realized it was Reggie's Audi that was smashed into the large oak tree. It was folded like paper; the entire hood was bent like an accordion. I slammed on brakes and jumped out of the car.

"Ma'am! Ma'am! Get back in your car!" one of the officers yelled.

"That's my husband! Reggie! Oh my God, Reggie!" I screamed as I ran toward the ambulance. I stumbled as I pressed my way through the officers. One of the men in black blocked my path. "Move! That's my husband!" I pushed passed him like I was a quarterback for the NFL. I pounded on the back doors, but the officers pulled me away and the ambulance sped off.

"Ma'am they're trying to save his life! Meet them at the hospital!"

I ran back to my car and ignored the honking from the other cars piled up behind me. "Oh God! Please let him be okay!" I prayed. Tears rolled down my eyes and everything suddenly seemed so pointless. The adultery, the arguing, everything. Nothing mattered to me other than Reggie. I sped like a bat out of hell and didn't even park the car when I arrived at the emergency room.

"I need to see my husband!" I yelled at the check-in nurse.

"Ma'am please calm down. What is his name?"

"Reggie! Reggie Montana!"

She typed his name into the computer. "We don't have anyone here by that name."

"He was in an accident! He was just brought in! I need to see him!"

"Okay." She clicked a few more buttons and read the screen. "It looks like he's in emergency surgery. As soon as they update his condition someone will be out to talk to you. You have to take a seat and fill these forms out while you wait." She handed me his medical history and insurance forms and I took a seat in the corner of the room.

"Ma'am is that your car?" The security officer pointed to my Benz. I nodded yes.

"You can't park there. You're gonna have to move it please."

I walked outside and moved my car in the closest parking space. I called Reggie's parents and told them to get to the hospital immediately. I also called Grace to check on the twins and informed her of what happened. I asked her not to tell them anything and that I would be checking in periodically for updates. I also remembered Daddy would be in need of assistance with his dinner, so I made arrangements for that as well.

"Daddy I'm not going to be able to come by this evening," I wept.

"Sadie baby what's wrong?" I could hear the concerning in his voice as my tears flowed.

"It's Reggie. I'm at the hospital, he was in an accident."

"Oh, dear God! Is he okay? What are the doctor's saying?"

"I just got here. They haven't told me anything except he's in surgery."

"It's going to be alright baby. Reggie's strong and a fighter. Whatever it is he's gonna pull through this. You just stay strong. You got them babies and this ain't the time to fall apart."

"I love you, Daddy."

"I love you too Sadie baby... hold on I have another call coming through," Daddy said before switching over to the other line.

I thought about the day I'd met Reggie. How he kept looking at me over his Spike Lee glass frames. He was so sweet to me and didn't deserve the pain I'd put him through. "God, I promise, I'll never do him wrong again if you just let him be alright. Please God," I begged.

"Sadie?"

"Yes, Daddy I'm still here."

"Things just got worse. The hospital called, and they said your brother is in there," he announced.

"What!"

"Yeah they just called and said that he was admitted about four hours ago. I need you to go check on your brother, Sadie."

"Oh, Lord! What happened?"

"They said he was dropped off at the hospital. It looks like he was beaten up pretty bad. Sadie, I know you're worried about Reggie, but I need you to go check on your brother for me."

"I'll call you back as soon as I know more." I ended the call and rushed back inside to talk with the nurse.

"Gabriel Tennan was admitted here a few hours ago. I need to know what room he's in."

"Room 222. Go through the double doors and take the first left. His room will be to the right of the nurse's station at the end of the hall," she informed.

"Thank you!" I took off down the hall and followed her directions. I opened the door as more tears seeped from my eyes. Gabriel was laying in the bed with his eyes closed. Partially because he was unable to open the left one. It was swollen shut and the size of a tennis ball. His mouth was busted and bloody with a tube coming out of his nose. I'd never seen him or anyone I loved in such bad condition.

Tap, tap tap. The door opened, and a white coat entered the room. "Hi I'm Dr. Kevorkian." He held his hand out, but I just stared at him in disbelief and he knew exactly why I felt uncomfortable. "I am of no relation I swear!" He held his hands up and crossed his heart with his finger.

"I'm sorry it's just,"—

112

"I know, I know. I'm getting another badge made that's going to say Dr. Kev."

"That would definitely be better." I sighed.

"How are you related to the patient?" he asked.

"I'm his sister. Someone called my father to inform him that he was here, but he's disabled so he told me."

"I understand. We'll your brother was dumped outside of the hospital. A black van pulled up and threw him out in the parking lot then drove off. He's been beaten pretty badly as you can see. He has three broken ribs and all of his fingers on his right hand his broken. He had a dislocated shoulder as well as multiple contusions all over his body. The tube is in place because one of the broken ribs punctured his lung. Whoever did this to you brother wanted him to suffer."

"They wanted him to die!" I sobbed.

"They could have killed him if they wanted to, but they brought him here. His injuries are case specific. We have had several people admitted with highly similar injuries; especially the fingers being broken on the right hand only. We definitely think this is gang-related."

"Was there anyone admitted with him? A girl... Mercedes Viller." I needed to know what happened to Mercedes. I prayed she wasn't in any danger.

"No, I'm sorry. He was alone."

"Is he able to talk?"

"He can hear you and was aware of what's going on, but conversation would just be too painful at this point. We gave him some pretty strong meds to take the pain away so he's probably going to be out for a while anyway."

"Alright thank you doctor, also I was already here because my husband, Reggie Montana was in a car wreck. I was hoping to get an update on his condition."

"Reggie Montana..." Dr. Kev flipped through a small stack of papers he had under his arm. "He's still in surgery."

"Can you tell me what they are operating on specifically?"

"I'm not his doctor but I can have someone with more information come in here and talk to you."

"That would be great thanks." I shook his hand and he disappeared out the door.

CHAPTER 20

$\mathcal{I}$ pulled out my phone and tried to call Mercedes again. Voicemail. I called her parents and hoped she was at home.

"Hello," Pastor Viller answered cheerfully.

"Hello Pastor, this is Sadie. Is Mercedes available?"

"Hi Sadie and no I'm sorry to say she isn't. Did you call her phone?"

"Yes, I did but it keeps going to voicemail."

"Well would you like to leave a message for her?"

"Pastor, I think there may be something wrong."

"What do you mean, Sadie?"

"I met with Mercedes earlier to discuss her nanny position and I had my brother with me"—

"Hold on a minute. I think that's her now. Mercedes! Is that you?" he called out. "Sadie Montana is on the phone for you." He handed her the phone.

"Hello?" Mercedes answered, and I felt the stress release from my shoulders, some of it anyway.

"Oh, thank God!" A huge sigh of relief left my body. "I've been calling your phone and I got worried when the doctor said you didn't arrive with my brother," I rambled.

"What doctor? Why are you at the hospital?" she sounded puzzled.

"Gabriel! I don't know what happened, but he's been beaten pretty badly. I thought you were caught up in it somehow. You have no idea how relieved I am to know you're safe." I began crying on the phone. With everything crumbling around me, this was a brief moment of happiness.

"Oh my gosh, I had no idea. He and I talked for a while longer, but then he got a phone call. It seemed pretty serious. He said it was work related and that he had to make some moves but he'd be in touch with me because he wanted to take me out," she revealed.

"Work-related?" I knew exactly what that meant. "Alright well thank you Mercedes. I'm really glad you're safe." I ended the call not revealing what happened to Reggie. I needed to know my husband was at least stable before informing outsiders. I thought about telling the pastor, but I wasn't super religious, and I only went to church because Miriam insisted. The only people that had a right to know was his parents regardless of what drama we were going through. I looked over at Gabe and noticed his eyes were fluttering like he was trying to open them. I rushed over and grabbed his right hand. "Gabriel! Can you hear me?"

He cracked his left eye open as far as he could and I felt him squeeze my hand. He could hear me, and he knew I was there.

"Oh, Gabe what have you gotten yourself into? I cried. I kissed his hand as the tears continued to flow. I didn't care about the past and how bad he may have treated when we were younger. I loved my brother and he didn't deserve to be laying in a hospital bed beaten like this. "Who did this to you? I promise on Mommy I'll get whoever did this to you!"

He tried to speak, but the tube running down his nose and throat prevented that.

"No don't try to speak. Just relax."

He squeezed my hand again to acknowledge he understood. I grabbed the pen and notepad that was sitting beside the telephone. I took the cap off and placed it in his hand with the pad underneath. "Who did this to you?" I demanded.

He took his time, but successfully wrote the name Bishop.

"I knew it!" My suspicions were correct. Bishop was the greasiest muthafuckah on the southside. He made a living off the backs of young girls. Mainly run-aways between the ages of sixteen and twenty. He wasn't your regular old pimp prostituting chicks out though. He only recruited the ones considered top notch to service his upscale clientele. These young women could have easily been models in someone's magazine or walking down a catwalk, but instead he fed on their insecurities and had them sucking and fucking these upper-middle-class white men for his come up; not to mention he provided them with their drug of choice when they called him to set up a party. I took the pen out of Gabe's hand, but he tapped the pad signaling he wasn't finished writing. I placed the black ballpoint back into his fingers and he began to scribble more words. He dropped the pen when he was finished and looked at me while grab-bing my hand.

"Gabriel what are you talking about?" I asked as I read the childlike scribble.

mercedes danger

I threw the pad on the bed. "Mercedes is fine. I just talked to her. She's safe at home with her parents."

He let go of my hand and pounded his pointer finger on the pad several times. The way he beat that pad let me know he was serious.

"Oh, Gabe what have you done?" I sighed

"So-rry Sa-die," crept from his lips in the frailest whisper. He closed his eye as a single tear escaped then turned his head away from me.

I walked out of the room and headed toward the waiting room thinking of how I was going to tell the Pastor and his wife that Mercedes might be in possible danger because of me when I heard a familiar shrill coming from around the corner.

"I DEMAND TO SEE HIM RIGHT NOW!" Miriam's voice was louder than New York traffic. I turned the corner and saw her waving her crunchy Cheeto like finger in the intake nurse's face.

"Ma'am if you don't calm down I will have security remove you!" the nurse reprimanded.

"Miriam calm down. There is nothing we can do but wait!" Reggie Sr. pulled his wife away from the desk and pushed her onto a chair. A look of relief came over his worried face when he saw me walking towards them.

"Reggie, Miriam," I acknowledged their presence as I took a seat directly across from them.

"Did the Doctors tell you anything about his condition yet?" Reggie Sr. questioned.

"No, they haven't told me anything either." I sighed.

"This is all your fault!" Miriam sat up in her chair, staring at me like she was a damn zombie.

"Miriam I am not dealing with ANY of your shit today! My husband, your son, is in there fighting for his life and this is the type of shit you want to pull right now? I just found out my brother is here as well and in bad condition so today is NOT the mutha-fuckin' day! If you think I'mma take any more shit from your miserable ass, just try me you old bitch, and everyone you know will be visiting you in one of these hospital beds!" I stared her down like an eagle on a rat and meant every fucking word I said. I was prepared to slide her foul-mouth-ass across this floor and explain my provoked actions to Reggie later. She fixed her crooked lips to say something, but Reggie Sr. cut her off.

"Now that's enough! Miriam leave Sadie alone and I mean right this instant. She didn't do anything. Their marriage problems aren't any different from most of the people in this damn town so to hell with images. If you want to blame someone blame me. I caused this. This is the result of my actions," Reggie Sr. said and placed his head down.

"Mr. and Mrs. Montana." A male nurse approached us.

"Yes?" Reggie Sr. answered and we all perked up in hopes of positive news about Reggie.

"On behalf of Kennedy Medical we'd like to offer you our private waiting area. We appreciate your contribution to our facility," he continued.

"I want to know about my son!" Miriam blurted.

"Mrs. Montana, we understand your concern, but there really isn't anything that I'm authorized to tell you as of right now. Please be assured that our top surgeon, Paul Makowski is working to make sure your son has the best care. Our staff is dedicated to doing everything we can to provide you with maximum comfort in this needed time."

Surprisingly Miriam accepted his well-rehearsed statement and followed him as he guided us to a very spacious and well accommodated waiting area. Having money definitely made a difference because there were other people waiting on their loved ones to come out of surgery and they weren't offered the same treatment. After about ten minutes of complete silence, I was reminded that I needed to call my father.

"I'm sorry about your brother," Miriam spoke softly. "I'm sorry about everything." She wept.

I walked out of the room and dialed my father. "Daddy, Gabe was beaten pretty bad, but the doctor said he's expected to make a full recovery. Everything is just a waiting game at this point." I talked with my father a little while longer, making sure he had the information about the chef and any direct numbers to my assistants if he needed anything. I ended the call and decided to get clarity about what happened after I left Mercedes and Gabriel at the restaurant.

"Hello," Mercedes answered.

"Hey Mercedes, I was wondering if you can tell me exactly what happened after I left. I'm trying to figure out who could have done this to my brother. He's unable to tell me anything at this point," I lied. It's not that I didn't trust Mercedes, I just didn't want to reveal anything to anyone yet.

"Um, it's like I told you. He got a phone call, took it in the restroom and when he came out he started acting real nervous like."

"Did he use my car service to get home?"

"No, I volunteered to take him. It was the least I could do for him saving my life."

"Are you sure you took him home?"

"Yeah he said it was his house. Why?"

"I'm asking because my father hadn't seen him in a day. So, I'm sure he had you drop him off somewhere else."

"*Um,* hold on let me see. I added it to my GPS, so I could get home."

I waited while Mercedes retrieved the GPS location.

"2794 Vander-Beek Drive."

"That's not his house. Was anyone outside standing around when you pulled up?"

"Yeah it was two guys talking in the front yard. I think he called one Phillip or something."

"Bishop," I said under my breath.

"Yeah, yeah I think it was Bishop."

"Okay, well listen to me. Stay away from him. I believe he is the one that did this to Gabe. He's bad news," I spoke sternly.

"I understand. I don't know what he'd want with me anyway. I just dropped Gabriel off and that was it."

"I understand, but you never know with these types. Just be mindful of your surroundings. I don't trust any of those grimy mutha fuckahs." I ended the call with Mercedes and walked back into the waiting room. I needed to know what was weighing so heavily on my husband that he lost control of his car.

CHAPTER 21

"What did you and Reggie talk about?" I asked Reggie Sr. directly. I wasn't going to beat around the bush. Clearly there was a lot that Reggie didn't know and he became over-whelmed when he found out.

"Everything." Reggie Sr. looked over at Miriam as she rolled her eyes in disgust. "I'm not proud of my actions over the years, but I'm still his father."

"His father, her father, their father…" Miriam's words trailed.

"How many are there?" I questioned.

"Three. Isaiah, Lilly and Nathaniel. All different mothers, all different states. All taken care of and provided for."

"You say it as if it makes it any better," Miriam hissed.

"I kept them out of our lives because that's what YOU wanted Miriam. Hell, you demanded it. These were your cover-ups that I went along with because you said you couldn't bare anyone knowing the truth."

"You're damn right I didn't want anyone knowing that you'd pissed on our marriage!"

"Oh, Miriam cut the shit! If we are going to be transparent tell the whole damn truth! You think I don't know about your rendezvous with Quinton? You think I haven't had you followed to that hotel room you sneak off to every third Thursday of the month? I figured after all I put you through you deserved for someone to make you happy. To make you smile. I sure as hell can't do it." Reggie Sr's words left a shocking silence in the air. Miriam looked as if an alien had walked into the room.

"How long have you known?" Miriam asked.

"From the first time it happened. I know you better than you know yourself, woman. I knew that once you found out about Isaiah it would only be a matter of time before you sought your own revenge, and I was right. Three months later I had photos on my desk of you and that bastard. I could have torn him limb from limb, but I figured I deserved it for what I'd did to you both."

"What did you do to him?" I asked. I figured if they were in the sharing mood I might as well get all the tea and I was parched. I'd take a full glass with two sugars.

"I took his business. We were partners. When I first started out it was Quinton that gave me a chance and taught me the ropes. Not the shit you learn in college, but the real insider's information you gain by knowing the right people. I watched him like a hawk and learned how he made power moves on people, slowly taking over their businesses. The only problem was he was becoming careless. He allowed his success to get to his head and the quality of his work started slipping. You can only mess with wealthy people's money so many times before they start looking elsewhere; when they did decide it was time to find new advisors, I was there to assure them that I was nothing like Quinton Shields. I was his protégé, but I was better. It didn't take but a few power moves of my own and next thing he knew the entire company was being run by me. I pushed him out of the business he started and turned it into a multi-million-dollar company. I bought out his shares and that's how the Montana Corp. was founded."

"And what about LaNoir? How'd that happen?" I polled, remembering the look on Brookyln's face when LaNoir revealed Reggie Sr. was Nathaniel's biological father.

Reggie Sr. sighed and rubbed his hands through his curly salt and pepper stands. Overlooking the bloodshot eyes he had from crying, he really was a very handsome man. Combine that with wealth and power it's a wonder if he didn't have a child in every state and foreign country. "I had a little too much to drink at your engagement party. LaNoir was highly intoxicated as well. One flirt lead to another and we ended up in bed together before the weekend was out."

"But Nathaniel looks around the same age as Chandler and Josiah."

"That's because he couldn't sleep with the Jezebel one time and leave it at that. No, he had to make an ongoing thing." Miriam's pain enunciated her words perfectly.

"Nathaniel is six," Reggie Sr. mumbled. There was a moment of silence right before we heard a tap on the door.

"Mr. and Mrs. Montana, I'm Dr. Makowski, the head surgeon here at Kennedy. I performed your son's surgery and he's currently stable, but he's going to need a blood transfusion."

Everyone's eyes widened as the doctor spoke. "Well what are you waiting on. Do it!" Miriam belted.

"That's the problem. Your son is O negative which means he can only receive blood from someone who is also O negative, and we just don't have that available. Because of the tragedy that occurred when the stadium collapsed last month, we are short in all areas and slowly rebuilding."

"Well we are his parents can't you just use some of ours?" Reggie Sr. suggested.

"We've already compared your records on file and..." the doctor's words faded. He looked over at Miriam.

"And we are not a match," she finished his sentence.

"Well how can that be? I'm his father and she's his mother," Reggie Sr. searched the doctors face for answers.

"Because you're not his father," I blurted out. It didn't take a rocket scientist to figure out he was not the father.

"I'll give you a few minutes to talk. I realize this is a life-changing situation, but we need to find a match as soon as possible. We are reaching out to blood centers and other hospitals, but they are in the same boat as we are." Dr. Makowski exited the room and all eyes were on Miriam.

She walked over to her bag and retrieved the phone from her purse then headed for the door.

"Where the fuck do you think you're going!" Reggie held the door closed with his hand. He was enraged and fuming.

"To call Quinton," Miriam pushed his hand out of the way and went out into the hall.

"What have I done?" Reggie Sr. cried. "This is all my fault!" He dropped to his knees, sobbing hard and uncontrollably. I went over trying to provide him some comfort, but how do you soothe a man who just found out that his son isn't his? Roughly twenty minutes had passed before Miriam returned looking more disheveled than before.

"Sadie can you excuse us." She walked over to Reggie. "I need to talk to my husband."

I left the room and went to go check on Gabe. He was sleeping as expected so I just sat in the chair beside him and thought about everything that happened leading up to this point. They say everything that happens in the dark eventually comes to the light, but in times like these I wonder if it's best that some secrets should remain. Why do we stay in committed relationships, no longer fulfilling our needs? Seeking validation from outside sources when we could put that same effort into our own relationship. Are we so afraid of being alone that staying through blatant disrespect is better than starting over? Even looking at my own transgressions, comfort wasn't enough to keep me from fantasizing about Brooklyn. When did we become so obsessed with how the world views us that we are willing to sacrifice our own happiness just to maintain a false image. When we log out of Facebook, when we stop posting on Instagram, when we stop lying for our significant other, and stop lying to ourselves to acknowledge the fact that we are not perfect and we all have room for improvement, then and only then can we begin to heal from this seemingly repeated cycle of abuse we force ourselves to be in.

My mother use to say, "An old fool wasn't nothing but a young fool at one time." We keep up these false appearances to somehow validate our worth by what others view as success. Staying in a fading relationship slowly kills you inside. You become a shell of your former self and you really are no longer the same by the time you are willing to say aloud, "It's over."

Most men live by 'it's cheaper to keep her,' while causing so much emotional damage that their significant other isn't fit to have a loving, trusting relationship after they've finally realized it's time to move on. Women will follow their mom's logic of 'standing by your man,' and produce more generations of bitter and broken women, nagging and belittling their mate and sacrificing their own happiness just to have a perfect family photo on Christmas; making everyone miserable in reality. This bullshit has to change, and I knew it had to start with me. As hard as it was to reveal my truths, I knew it was necessary to heal my damaged relationship. I'm just grateful Reggie was willing to forgive me, and I, him. Marriage is more than a piece of paper. It's knowing that you love this person so much that you are willing to trust having your own life decisions made by them if you no longer have that option, and I would do anything to save my husband.

I stayed in the hospital for almost two weeks straight keeping an eye one both Reggie and Gabe. I was finally talked into going home to ease my mind once I knew both were in the clear. I did need to handle some things concerning my business and the boys personal care because I still didn't have a nanny for them and I knew I needed to give Grace a raise for stepping up to the plate. I did what I thought was best and called Mercedes.

"I'm sorry about Mr. Montana and your brother, but I'm not going to be able to keep the boys," Mercedes informed.

"Oh, I'm sorry to hear that."

"It's not personal. I love Josiah and Chandler, but I have a business opportunity that I've decided to pursue."

"Really? Well that's great. If there's anything I can help you with let me know. I really hate the way things turned out and I honestly wish you the best Mercedes."

"Thank you so much."

"May I ask what your new venture is?"

"KB Productions. I was offered a modeling contract and I jumped right on it."

"Wow, that sounds amazing. I'm happy for you. Did you have your parents look over the contract before signing?

"No offense, but I'm grown. I don't need my parent's permission to make my own career choices. Besides Daddy doesn't see modeling as a real career. I've had other opportunities in the past, but he would never allow me to pursue them."

"I wasn't trying to offend you. I just think it's best to have someone go over anything dealing with a contract."

"I know how to read and comprehend." Mercedes tone was turning salty.

"That's not what I was... just promise me you'll at least get at lawyer to look over it before you finalize anything. I really wish you much success." I ended the call and prayed she'd follow my advice. This generation was so hell-bent on doing things their way that they didn't realize that they could avoid the trouble we'd already gone through it they'd just listen to some solid advice.

CHAPTER 22

*G*abriel was released after his three-week bid in the hospital. "I'm ready to give this shit up," he told my father and I on his first day home. I couldn't tell if it was just the shock of going through a life or death experience, but he definitely came across as sincere.

"My offer still stands. Once you're completely healed I'll talk to some people about finding you a legit job making some decent money." I reminded him.

Reggie's recovery was slow both mentally and physically. After Quinton gave blood for his transfusion, Reggie Sr, Miriam and Reggie Jr. had to have a long, revealing, conversation of their own. It's amazing how we can openly judge someone for the same mistakes we choose to keep private. Miriam claimed she honestly didn't know that Quinton was Reggie's real father after revealing she'd been sleeping with him way before Reggie Sr. had caught on. As crazy as it all sounded, Reggie Sr. seemed to show his love for Miriam with his actions this time as opposed to the monetary things he provided. They decided to lay everything out on the table in therapy. No more lies, no more secrets, no more cover-ups of the truth. They even decided to try to form a real relationship with Reggie's other siblings.

A few months passed since the car crash and Reggie was doing better every day due to his intense therapy. Hearing you may never walk again was the motivation he needed to actively prove the doctors wrong.

Brooklyn moved out of his home the night of the blow-up, and even with LaNoir pleading with him to come back home, he said he just didn't see that happening any time soon. He stayed an active father to Nathaniel who was doing much better now that Reggie Sr. stepped up to be in his life. He received top-notch care and was delighted to meet his identical twin nephews even though they didn't quite understand how they were basically the same age as their uncle. In time all things would gain clarity, but for now we all were focused on our own lives; repairing the shattered pieces of ourselves in hopes to be a better mate for one other.

"Hello," I answered the phone, in hopes that Gabe had good news. After he got the cast off of his hand I set him up with an interview at one of my soros's security agency. Gabriel was six-three, two hundred and thirty pounds of muscle. This would be a perfect job for him.

"I got the job!" he announced proudly.

"Yay! I'm so proud of you!"

"Yeah I start on Monday and I'll get full benefits after my trial period."

"See I knew you could do it. You got this!"

"Shit, I got this because of you. I know I wasn't always the brother you needed me to be but thank you Sadie." I could feel his smile through the phone. "Aye, whatever happened to that lil' chocolate drop? Shit a nigga 'bout to be makin' some real paper now. Maybe I can treat her to a proper date," Gabriel inquired.

"Who Mercedes? She's been gone for a couple months now. She got a modeling contract and relocated to New York, I think."

"A modeling contract? Damn that's what's up. Who she get her shit through?"

"Why you tryna be a model?" I laughed.

"I mean shit, a nigga is handsome," he boasted.

"Yeah, but you're past your prime," I joked.

"Ha, ha. I see you got jokes."

"Nah, but I think she said something about KC, KB Productions or something like that. I really can't remember."

"Did you say KB Productions?" Gabe's voice cracked.

"Yeah I think that was it. Why?"

"Fuck! KB Productions is a bullshit cover up business for King Bishop. He got her Sadie. She's in the game now."

To be continued...

NOTES FROM THE AUTHORESS

"We must find time to stop and thank the people who make a difference in our lives"
-John F. Kennedy.

I hope you enjoyed reading this story as much as I did writing it. I stayed up late plenty of nights excited by how it was unfolding. I honestly believe most people deserve a 2nd chance to prove that we all have room to grow if we can acknowledge our mistakes and truly embrace that we aren't perfect but striving to be a better version of who we were yesterday. Life is a roller coaster, when your down it's only a matter of time before you go back to the top, but you must be willing to ride the wave to get there. Thank you to my new readers who's supported my books. Each one has a different place in my heart and I'm glad that I can share them with you. If you like my work (s) please leave me a review and don't be afraid to hit me up on social media; I'd love to hear from you.

To my Curvy Girl Crew- Thank you isn't enough for the love you've shown. Every shared post, every comment, every like, and all the words of encouragement hasn't gone unnoticed. I'm excited to call you my pen sisters and I love watching our growth as a unit. You are greatly appreciated.

I am truly grateful to have some of the most amazing people in my life that I can call on when I need encouragement, inspiration, or just to share a laugh. You've supported my dreams by helping me achieve my goals with your positive thoughts, uplifting words and monetary support. Even to my test readers who provide me with honest feedback, I want to say thank you! I truly appreciate your presence in my life and want you to know you are never forgotten but placed highly in my heart.

Beulah's Babies

Spencer Willis

Barry BSmooth Vereen

Nneka Bolds

Jason "Swizzy" Irby

Shemeeka Stampp

Shanikia Hill

Kelley McMillion

Nathanael Washington

Jasmine Jo Owens

Tiffany "Tip" Herbin

Nina Evans

Robert McGhee

ABOUT THE AUTHOR

Sunni Nykohl (37) is a Greensboro, NC native and is a graduate of Virginia College of Greensboro where she obtained a license in cosmetology. She has been a featured makeup artist for local shows and specializes in natural hair design. Sunni Nykohl has written many short stories but decided to dive into the romantic arts by writing her 1st published piece 'Seduction of a Savage' and completing the 3 arch series this year. She is also featured in Curves of Destruction Volume 2 with her short-story, Three-Way. This mother of 3 looks forward to sharing her fantasy world with her readers with more books to come.

If interested in supporting this Curvy Girl's movement, please be sure to stay connected to Sunni Nykohl on

Fan Page- https://www.facebook.com/Sunninykohl1/
E-mail- sunninykohl@yahoo.com

facebook.com/SunniNykohl

instagram.com/sunni_nykohl

SUBMISSIONS

Curvy Girl Publications is accepting
submissions from experienced & aspiring authors
in the area of BBW Romance!

If interested in joining a successful, independent publishing company,
send the first 15K words/60 pages of your completed manuscript to
curvygirlpub@royaltypublishinghouse.com!

Submissions should be sent as a Microsoft Word document,
along with your synopsis, query letter and contact information.

Curvy Girl Publications is now accepting manuscripts from aspiring
or experienced BBW romance authors!

WHAT MAY PLACE YOU ABOVE THE REST:

Heroes who are the ultimate book bae: strong-willed, maybe a little
rough around the edges but willing to risk it all for the woman
he loves.

Heroines who are the ultimate match: the girl next door type, not
perfect - has her faults but is still a decent person. One who is willing
to risk it all for the man she loves.

The rest is up to you! Just be creative, think out of the box, keep it
sexy and intriguing!

If you'd like to join the Royal family, send us the first 15K words (60
pages) of your completed manuscript to submissions@royaltypublish-
inghouse.com

LIKE OUR PAGE!

Be sure to <u>LIKE</u> our Curvy Girl Publications page on Facebook!